THE SIGN

Robin Maugham

A STAR BOOK
published by
W. H. ALLEN

A Star Book
Published in 1975
by W. H. Allen & Co. Ltd.
A division of Howard & Wyndham Ltd.
44 Hill Street, London W1X 8LB

First published in Great Britain by
W. H. Allen & Co. Ltd. 1974

Copyright © Robin Maugham 1974

Printed in Great Britain by
Richard Clay (The Chaucer Press), Ltd., Bungay, Suffolk

ISBN 0 352 39829 9

THE SIGN

Some reviews of the hardcover bestseller

For Christopher

PART ONE

All these events occurred in the year which eventually became known as AD 20.

In that year Valerius Gratus was the Governor of the country called by the Romans Palestine – Valerius Gratus, not Pontius Pilate, who succeeded him.

In AD 20, John the Baptist had not begun his ministry and it would be at least ten years before Jesus began his.

Jesus was one of a long line of prophets and visionaries who had been inspired by the Essene teachings. This is the story of what happened to one of his predecessors. The character of Jesus does not appear in this work.

PART TWO

CHAPTER ONE

In the far distance two fishermen are calling to each other across the lake. Sometimes, in a fit of sentimentality, I envy the simple lives the fishermen who live in the little village below our villa seem to lead. I say 'seem' because I am certain their lives may be as filled with doubts and worries as mine is. If I were a true poet I should know. But I have reached the age of thirty, and I am aware that the gift has not yet come to me.

I am still only half awake. I can hear the doves cooing in the courtyard. From the servants' quarters I can listen to Leah giving instructions to the new girl we have employed to help work in the kitchen. Leah, in fact, manages the whole household, and that is what Joseph wants – though as his secretary and companion I should, I suppose, be in charge. But from the very first week that I came as a young man to live with Joseph he insisted I should have plenty of spare time to pursue may ambition to become a poet.

It is time I got out of bed. Yet who would care if I stayed in bed all day? Joseph has his first meal of the day alone in his room, and he would not notice my absence for another two hours. Then, when he was told by one of the servants – Manasseh perhaps – that I was still in my room, he would think it his duty to come and visit me. If I told him the truth, if I said I had no desire to leave my bed because I knew that the day held nothing in store for me, Joseph would immediately become solicitous. I can picture the look of concern on his sleek, handsome face; I can observe the wrinkles on his forehead; I can see his delicate hand rising to stroke back a strand of his grey hair; I can hear the faint tone of distress which he would infuse into his resonant voice. I say 'infuse' because, of course, only a part of him – the part governed by his conscience and his incongruously strict principles – would be worried by my behaviour. The other half of him would be calculating rapidly what action he should take to keep a friend with whom he was once in love – a friend who was still a useful companion

13

and secretary. He might, for instance, suggest that we should move for a while to another of his properties in the land. To Jericho, perhaps. But if I suggested that we could join one of his camel caravans and travel to Egypt, the lines of his face would shift as he invented an easy reason why such a journey would be impossible. For Joseph has a small house on the harbour-front of Alexandria, but he has never allowed me to accompany him on any journey to Egypt, and I can guess the reason why. His care for his reputation does not extend beyond the frontiers of Israel.

Yet why should I have awakened this morning in such a discontented mood? What have I to complain about? I live in security and comfort; I do not need to worry about money; I have leisure; I have servants to wait upon me; I eat and drink well. Most important of all, I love the man who employs me. Perhaps therein lies the root of my discontent. For Joseph no longer loves me; I doubt if he ever did. Joseph is extremely kind to me. But the truth is that in spite of his kindness Joseph has used me purely to suit his own convenience, and today in a different fashion he is still using me.

When Joseph met me I was seventeen. As a boy I wasn't particularly vain, but I knew I was attractive: I knew it by the way people looked at me. Joseph first saw me across a long room at an evening party in Jerusalem. He asked our host to introduce us. Joseph was wearing a dark-blue velvet robe, I remember. He looked tall and distinguished. He was then thirty-two years old, but already his face was lined, and there were streaks of grey in his hair and in his well-trimmed beard. As we stood talking to each other, his movements were casual, and his smile was almost indifferent. But from his eyes I could see that in his mind he was taking off my tunic and imagining me naked. Later that evening he took me to his house where he lived alone, and we sat in chairs, covered with silk he had brought back from Alexandria, which were placed beneath an awning on the roof. As we gazed at the stars and drank our wine he made me tell him of the death of my father and mother in Hebron and, presently, of my ambition to become a poet. As I now spoke to him, he was staring at me intently. His hand as he lifted his glass to drink was trembling. Towards dawn, he told me that he had fallen in love with me. And I believed him – because I wanted to believe him. My parents were dead. I had little money. More important, inside me I felt a great need to love someone like Joseph. And I wanted him to love me.

As dawn was breaking Joseph led me to his room. That evening occurred twelve years ago.

At first I was wonderfully happy. Each day seemed to sparkle with my joy. Joseph seemed as joyful as I was and as passionate. The months turned slowly into years and still our contentment did not diminish – in spite of differences that existed between us. For, of course, there were differences. One of these most certainly was – and still is – our conflicting attitudes towards the Roman forces of occupation. Joseph's father had been a strict Pharisee who detested the presence of the Romans in our land, who abominated their idols, who resented their restrictions, who longed with all his soul for independence. And though when I first met Joseph he did not appear to be seriously interested in politics, gradually, as the years passed by, I noticed that he was spending more time with our politicians in Jerusalem. Even so I was surprised when he became a member of our High Council, the Sanhedrin. From that moment I observed he was less willing to discuss politics with me, and it was only from chance remarks I realized that Joseph in his turn was now beginning to be filled with hatred for the Romans, and I sensed that he was disappointed I could not share his attitude.

'But after all,' I would say to Joseph, 'what are the facts? Our country is protected by the might of Rome from invasions from the North or South and from the marauding Arab tribes in the desert to the East. We Jews are exempt from conscription to military service, and we pay fewer taxes than almost any country in the world. Just as I am protected by your position and wealth,' I would say to Joseph, 'so is our land protected from a hostile world.'

'But Raguel,' Joseph would answer, his sonorous voice as quiet and benign as ever. 'My dear Raguel, you are thinking only in material terms. Our country – Palestine, as the Romans call it – may enjoy security and a measure of prosperity under this foreign occupation. But the fact remains that the foreigners who strut so confidently through the streets of our towns are the enemies of our nation. For all their protestations of friendship with some of our people, in their hearts they despise us thoroughly. Far worse, by all kinds of methods, openly and secretly, they are trying to destroy our spirit. Why? Because they are the enemy of God.'

When Joseph spoke in this unusually serious manner I would know I must remain silent, for we were approaching the dangerous area of the second gulf that divided us. From childhood Joseph had believed devoutly in God. Even after he had become completely aware of the fixed, unalterable inclination of his desires, even when he knew that each fulfilment of his passion was a sin, Joseph still believed in his religion. He considered that his form of love was unlawful; he felt guilty for committing a sin. Yet Joseph still sinned – and sinned ardently. Perhaps this division between his conscience and his passions may account for the deviousness of Joseph's nature. The fact remains that Joseph is religious – and I am not.

In my childhood I, too, trusted in God. But when I saw the plague of dysentery, which had spread from Egypt, attack first my darling mother and then my father, hard-working and honest lawyer that he was, when I saw each of them die in filth and agony, then I found it hard to believe in a God who was all-powerful and just. And I slipped away from my faith as a serpent from its skin.

Today I believe in only one thing – the love that I still feel for Joseph. I love him; I suppose I shall always love him. But I am no longer seventeen: I am thirty. I am no longer a smooth-skinned boy with supple limbs. Time has sharpened my features. Time has dulled the gold of my hair and the blue of my eyes. Time has dried up the spring of my happiness and tarnished my spirit. So Joseph no longer desires me. It is as simple as that. From his deep kindness Joseph pretends that the reason he now does not wish to make love to me is because of a strange alteration that has taken place in him and diminished the intensity of his passion. Certainly I have never seen Joseph show the slightest interest in any boy or young man we have met. He respects my feelings to that extent. But he still makes an occasional journey to Egypt with one of his caravans. I suppose I should be grateful that at least I do not know the identity of the young lover whom I suspect Joseph keeps in Alexandria. There is neither a face nor a form on whom I can fix my jealousy. But the danger still remains. One day Joseph may meet another boy of seventeen. The boy may attract him as strongly as I did long years ago. And then how would I manage to control my bitterness? I might even have to fight for my position as secretary. I remind myself that Joseph has always been loyal to me – even if he has been unfaithful. But I believe that Joseph has altered.

Sometimes I try to make myself think it is only my imagination which leads me to suppose that Joseph's whole character has changed.

Yet I cannot help being aware that he has become far more reserved in his conversation with me. In some odd way he has become withdrawn, secretive almost. At first I thought that perhaps some member of the Sanhedrin might from malice have made private charges against Joseph because of his close relationship with me. Yet we have lived together for twelve years as master and secretary, and there has been no scandal. So surely, now I am thirty it is most unlikely that anyone would pay attention to such a complaint. More recently, therefore, I have found myself wondering if Joseph has not begun to take after his father. And the implications of this thought disturb me most horribly. For Joseph's father went mad a few months before he died.

To drive away the frightening imaginings from my mind I now turn towards the window. Dan, my wizened little room-servant who comes from Capernaum and speaks Aramaic with the accent of the district, has drawn apart the curtains so I can see the balcony. The sun is shining brightly on to the irises and anemones I have planted, and beyond I can contemplate the dark blue water of the lake – the same colour as the robe Joseph wore the night I first met him. There is no wind today, and the rays of the sun glitter on the surface as if on a sheet of metal.

I will call Dan to prepare a bath for me. I will dress and go downstairs to begin my work for the day.

A few minutes after I had settled down in the main living-room, Leah came in with her shopping basket. She is a pleasant-looking woman in her early fifties, round-faced and stout, dependable and sincere. But sometimes I wonder if her placid manner does not conceal some deep passion. But *what* passion? I know Leah is very devout, so perhaps it is a yearning for some religious experience. Or is it a simple desire to find herself a husband before it is too late? I suppose I shall never know. I am fond of Leah – mainly because of her devotion to Joseph, which I find all the more remarkable when I remember that Joseph was unwittingly the cause of the deformity of her right arm. When Joseph was fifteen he developed a passionate interest in chemistry. He was boiling up a flagon of olive oil over the flame of a lamp. And Leah, one of his father's maids, was standing beside him, watching the beginning of the boy's experiment. Suddenly the flagon burst, and the boiling oil spurted out and poured over Leah's arm. It was a miracle that Joseph was unhurt. A doctor was immediately sent for, and Leah's arm was treated. But the oil must have destroyed some nerve, for she has never been able to use her arm since. Yet never once did she blame young Joseph. Never once did she complain. Leah nearly always looks cheerful. But this morning I noticed that she appeared worried. After I had paid her the money she needed for the morning's shopping in the market-place, I discovered the reason why she seemed vexed.

'There's something I should tell you, Master Raguel,' she announced. Leah calls both Joseph and me 'master' because she has known us since we were young; she has got into the habit, and there is nothing we can do about it.

'I was up early this morning,' Leah continued. 'So I decided I'd make a list of all the plates we've got stored in the chest. It's been on my mind for some time. I went through each piece most carefully, and I have to tell you that there's a plate missing from the nice set of silver you and Master Joseph brought back from Damascus.'

'It's impossible,' I pointed out. 'The chest is kept locked, and you have one key, and I have the other.'

'That's just it,' Leah replied. 'I can't understand the whole thing – unless I could have left it unlocked for a few moments, and someone took their opportunity.'

'Who would?' I asked. 'Who in this household?'

'The new girl we've taken on,' Leah answered. 'I don't trust little Merab. She's a sly one.'

'But Merab is only a child,' I protested. 'She can't be more than sixteen.'

'Seventeen,' Leah replied grimly. 'All of seventeen.'

'I am sure the plate will turn up somewhere,' I said soothingly – because at all costs I wanted to avoid trouble in the household. 'Besides, what would a girl like that do with a silver plate?'

'Sell it,' Leah replied. 'There are dishonest men in the village, the same as in any other. And a man who hasn't God in his heart will stoop to dishonesty – or so the new preacher says.'

'What preacher?' I asked in order to change the subject.

'Caleb.'

'Who is Caleb?' I enquired.

'He's the young preacher who has come to the village,' Leah answered. 'They say he's a prophet.'

'Not another one!' I exclaimed, laughing. 'Recently Galilee seems to have become infested by so-called prophets.'

'Now don't you laugh, Master Raguel,' Leah said. 'For all you and I know this one may be as true a prophet as the blessed Elijah. Already he's got quite a following. Anyhow I'm going to listen to him preach if I get my shopping done in time.'

As Leah spoke, Manasseh came in. He was carrying a small table, obviously newly made, with a single drawer in it. Manasseh is a powerfully built man of about sixty, with a stern, worn face. I try to like Manasseh for Joseph's sake. But the man is so serious and so deeply religious that he makes me feel uncomfortable: he reminds me I have lost my faith. In his youth Manasseh had been a servant of Joseph's father. In those days he was a Zealot who believed that all Jews should band together to overthrow their Roman oppressors. Joseph's father was secretly sympathetic to the Zealot cause. Moreover, in his erratic way he had taken such a liking to Manasseh that the young servant was forgiven almost any transgression. When Joseph's father would grow angry with his son, Manasseh often dared to take the boy's side. As a result, Joseph now keeps Manasseh in his household from loyalty. He is supposed to be a general handyman and a guardian. But Manasseh's main interest – apart from religion and the remains of his Zealot ardour – lies in carpentry, and he spends most of his time sawing away in a shed in the back yard.

'Good morning, Master Raguel,' Manasseh said, putting down his table. 'Good morning, Leah.'

'It can't be another table,' Leah remarked.

'What do you think it is?' Manasseh grunted. 'A chair?'

'As if we hadn't enough already,' Leah muttered.

'Tables are always useful,' Manasseh told her. 'For those who've got any sense.'

Leah picked up her shopping basket and moved towards the door that led to the outer courtyard.

'And they make good firewood – for those who haven't,' Leah said and went out, closing the door behind her.

'It's early yet,' Manasseh said to me. 'Why is the woman in such a hurry?'

I smiled at him. 'I'm afraid it is a secret,' I announced solemnly.

'Tell me,' Manasseh replied. 'I'll keep it.'

'Leah wants to do her shopping early so that she has time to listen to some new preacher.'

'Good luck to her,' Manasseh said. 'If I had a silver button for every new preacher that has come to the village, I'd be rich enough to retire.'

Manasseh turned away and stood for a while examining the new table. 'How do you like it?' he asked.

'You are a fine carpenter,' Manasseh,' I told him. 'Where shall we put the table?'

'In the master's bedroom,' Manasseh answered.

'He has two there already,' I pointed out.

'This is only a small one,' Manasseh replied. 'But I have been working on it all week.'

I went over to the table. 'Shall we try it in the corner by the window?' I suggested.

Manasseh did not answer. His face was set in a scowl of obstinacy which I knew all too well. I lifted the table and carried it to the window. As I put the table down, I heard something rattle. I opened the drawer. Inside was a small wooden object. I could guess what it was. For a moment I hesitated. Then I stretched out my hand and took from the drawer a small wooden cross in the shape of a T. I looked at it in silence. I knew that to the Zealots the cross signified the hundreds of men who were crucified every month – every week almost – on the hill in Jerusalem. But of what use was the symbol? When the last insurrection failed the Zealot movement lost its power. What use was it to think that even at this moment some poor man might be stretched on a cross in agony?

'Oh, Manasseh,' I said ruefully, 'I thought you had stopped all this dismal brooding long ago.'

'It's just between Master Joseph and me,' Manasseh answered. 'You don't understand.'

'I understand only too well,' I said gently.

'I remind Master Joseph from time to time,' Manasseh explained.

'There is no need to remind him,' I said.

There was silence. For a while I wondered if it was worth while trying yet again to persuade Manasseh that the Zealot cause had failed once and for all. But I knew that the man was far too obstinate to listen. In the silence, the knock on the main door of the outer courtyard sounded quite loud. Manasseh went to see who it was. I put the wooden cross back in the drawer of the table and closed it.

'Morning,' I heard Manasseh call out.

'Good morning, Manasseh,' a voice answered. 'How are you?'

'Living,' Manasseh replied.

A moment later he came back into the room with Ben.

In a definitely innocent way, both Joseph and I are sincerely fond of Ben. He was a young boy when Joseph first brought me to this villa overlooking the Lake of Galilee – or, as I am told we shall soon have to call it, the Lake of Tiberius. I can remember Ben as he was over ten years ago when Joseph and I first saw him standing at the back door of the villa with his twine bag full of fish that he hoped to sell to the new occupants of the house. He had evidently come straight from the lake, and he was naked except for a length of cloth wound round his waist. Perhaps it was because of his nearly complete nakedness that as I looked at the boy I was conscious of his body before I became aware of his face. For a boy so young, his shoulders were already quite wide and his chest was deep, yet his waist was astonishingly slender. Somehow he seemed to possess a strange quality which reminded me of an untamed cub. Next, I noticed the thick tangled curls of brown hair clustered on his head, and the brightness of his eyes and the unevenness of his teeth, very white against his sunburnt skin as he smiled at us. We bought fish he had brought and offered the boy a glass of milk. He came in nervously as if he were afraid of being trapped. He was very shy, almost sullen. But he came back the next day with more fish, and gradually he became less uncomfortable in our presence. As the months passed by he began to confide in us: he would tell us about the fishing-boat that belonged to his father, and one day in halting phrases he told us about a girl of his own age called Rachel who lived in the village and whom he hoped to marry when he was grown up.

By this time I suspected that Joseph was attracted to the boy. I also knew that he would do nothing about it – not only for my sake and the sake of his reputation, but because Ben was very young and obviously both innocent and honest. However, a year later, after some discussion between us, Joseph offered to send Ben to school to be educated.

Ben shook his head and grinned at us.

'Thanks,' he said. 'It's very kind of you. But what do I want with a school? I'm happy with my life as it is. Besides, they'd never make a scholar of me.'

'I understand,' Joseph told him. 'I understand and respect your judgment.'

From that moment onwards Ben would come up to the villa whenever he had any time to spare. Both Joseph and I enjoyed his company and high spirits and the sight of his growing beauty. Both of us knew we would never lay a finger on him.

When Joseph became a member of the Sanhedrin, he and I began to return together more often to his house in Jerusalem. We now came to Galilee less frequently. On each visit Ben would appear, and because we had not seen him for several months we would be amazed by the speed at which the boy seemed to have grown. And now, at twenty, Ben was a man. His shoulders were heavy, the muscles of his arms were thick, and he gave me the impression of intense strength. The animal quality in him was now more pronounced. But mixed together with his toughness, there was a strange tenderness which never ceased to surprise us.

'Ben!' I cried out as he came into the room. 'How are you?'

'Very well,' Ben replied. 'And you?'

As always, Ben was a little constrained by Manasseh's presence.

'I am well,' I answered. 'How is your wife?'

'I don't expect he knows,' Manasseh blurted out.

'She is in good health,' Ben replied, ignoring Manasseh.

'I am glad to hear it,' Manasseh grunted. Then he gave me a brief nod of his head. 'I'll be in my shed if anyone wants me,' he announced and left the room.

Ben and I grinned at each other.

'Sit yourself down,' I said to Ben. 'Can I offer you something to drink?'

'No thanks, Raguel,' Ben replied as he sat down beside me.

'Why has it been so long since you came to see us?' I enquired. 'Why have you left us for so many days without your fishes?'

'I have been away,' Ben answered.

'Where?'

Ben rubbed his hands together and was silent.

'What are you looking so worried about?' I asked.

'Nothing.'

'Then where have you been?'

'Out on the boat.'

'For the last three weeks?' I asked in surprise.

'I was fishing on the far side of the lake,' Ben told me.

'Leaving a beautiful young wife behind?' I said. 'Whatever made you stay away three weeks? Were you alone with your father?'

'No,' Ben answered, staring down at the mosaic floor as if he had never seen it before.

'Who *were* you with?'

'Caleb was with me part of the time,' Ben mumbled.

'Caleb?' I exclaimed. 'Caleb, the young preacher?'

'Yes.'

'How did you meet *him*?' I enquired.

'I was mending my net on the foreshore,' Ben explained. 'Caleb was preaching close by. So I strolled up to listen. He has a fine voice. Somehow he makes you believe almost every word he says. Afterwards I stayed behind, and I got talking to him.'

Once again Ben was silent.

'So then Caleb hired your boat?' I suggested.

Ben grinned at me. 'No,' he said. 'That's not how it happened.'

'Then what *did* happen?' I asked.

'Well, the next evening, after I'd come back with the catch I went to hear Caleb preach again. And once more I stayed behind and we got talking – for quite a while this time. And I suppose you could say we took a liking to each other. Or at any rate I took a liking to him.'

For an instant I was suspicious. I glanced towards Ben. His eyes were now shining as he watched me, and the expression on his face was so innocent that I realized that such an impure thought had never occurred to him.

'After a while we became quite close friends,' Ben continued. 'So I introduced him to Rachel and to my father and mother and to the rest of them down on the wharf. And most of them seemed to like him as much as I did. He's a wonderful man. He's been out in the boat several times. Sometimes he's used the boat to preach from when the crowds got too excited on the shore. And I'm proud to do what I can to help him. And I believe he trusts in me completely.'

'Are you trying to tell me you are now one of Caleb's followers?' I asked.

23

'Yes.'

'Is that why you have avoided coming to see us?'

Ben shifted his feet uneasily.

'No. I just haven't had time,' he answered. 'Even Rachel has been a little vexed with me.'

Ben looked all around the room, staring at the damascene carpets on the floor and at the ivory-inlaid chairs and at the white columns, as if searching for some object about which he could speak in order to change the drift of the conversation.

'How is your master?' he enquired.

'He will be pleased to see you,' I replied.

Ben gazed down at his hands.

'Why does he want to see Caleb?' Ben asked suddenly.

'Joseph wants to see Caleb?' I exclaimed. 'I cannot believe it.'

'I know!' Ben replied. 'I thought that would surprise you. But he sent word yesterday to Gomer.'

'Gomer!' I cried out. 'That crook! Do you mean to tell me that Gomer is also a disciple?'

Ben was amused; he no longer seemed nervous.

'Yes,' he answered. 'But at present only part-time.'

'And unpaid?'

'That's right,' Ben replied. 'In fact, he's even put money into our funds.'

I was astonished. Gomer is the kind of man you find in almost every village in this district. Gomer – for a fee, of course – is prepared to help you in every way he can. You want a servant; Gomer will find you one. You want to hire a boat; Gomer will provide it, complete with crew. You want to borrow money; Gomer, once he has established your credentials, will lend you as much as you need – at a high rate of interest. Gomer is fat and obsequious, yet, somehow, there is an endearing quality about him. I think it is a kind of wistfulness. I daresay it is this quality which has caused him to become one of Caleb's disciples. I have always rather liked Gomer. But for some reason, as soon as he moved into the district, Joseph took a dislike to the man's reputation, and he has always refused to meet him.

'What message did Joseph send?' I asked Ben.

'Manasseh came down early to the village and said he wanted to see our master up in the villa this morning.'

'I am supposed to be Joseph's secretary,' I said, a little bitterly, I

24

must confess. 'But now I seem to be the last person to know what is happening in the house.'

As I spoke Ben rose from his chair. I turned around. Joseph had come into the room. To judge from his smile he had evidently listened to my little complaint with amusement. It is true that we can never see those with whom we live daily with detachment. For once, I tried to examine Joseph as he might appear to a stranger. Such a stranger would obviously see a well-dressed, cultured man in his middle age, above medium height, whose lined face expressed both good humour and a certain aloofness. Here, the stranger would think, is a jovial man who is both benign and calm. As Joseph stood there smiling at Ben and at me his features were tranquil, and the stranger would not be able to observe the odd, hectic look which sometimes came into his eyes.

'Hullo, Ben,' Joseph said in his resonant voice. 'I am delighted to see you.' Then he turned to me. 'And what *is* happening in the house?' he asked.

'Why have you asked this Caleb of all people to come here?'

' "Without telling me",' Joseph prompted.

'Yes,' I replied. 'Without telling me.'

'I wanted it to be a surprise,' Joseph exclaimed. Then he looked towards Ben. 'Is he coming?'

'Yes,' Ben answered.

'Good,' Joseph replied as he sat down in his usual chair by the empty fireplace. His eyes had begun to search Ben carefully, and he seemed pleased with the result of his examination, for he smiled once more. 'How are you, Ben?' he enquired. 'You look well. More handsome that ever, I would say.'

'I'm in good health and happy,' Ben answered.

'But his wife is not happy at all,' I told Joseph with a wink.

'I find that hard to believe,' Joseph said, gazing at Ben. 'I'm sure your wife has every reason to be content.'

'Ben has spent the last three weeks with this Caleb you are so anxious to meet,' I explained.

'Not "anxious",' Joseph corrected. ' "Interested" to meet.' He glanced towards the water of the lake. 'How strange!' he said to himself. 'Three weeks with Caleb.' Then he turned back to Ben. 'Caleb can only be a year or two older than you are – or so I gather,' he murmured.

'That's right,' Ben answered.

'Do you see him often?'

'When I can spare the time.'

'What is it that draws you to the man?'

Ben hesitated. The sullen look which I remembered when he was a child had come back into his face.

'I believe in Caleb's teachings,' Ben answered.

'Surely you are not one of his disciples?' Joseph asked.

I watched Ben's hands clench themselves together.

'Yes,' he replied. 'I am.'

Joseph's voice was still placid and indifferent. 'How many disciples are there?' he enquired.

'Eight of us – so far,' Ben replied.

'The Essenes arrange their cells in groups of twleve,' Joseph informed him. 'Perhaps your friend will do likewise.'

Ben looked towards the door. 'If you still want to see Caleb, I'd better be going,' he announced. 'You see, I will have to help him from the market-place.'

'Help him?' I asked.

'Help him through the crowds,' Ben explained. 'They surround him after he's been preaching, and sometimes they won't let him move. And he will do nothing to push them off. So we have to make a way for him.'

Ben opened the door. 'I will see you both later,' he said, and left.

For a while Joseph and I were silent as we stared at each other, each trying to guess the other's thoughts. Such moments have occurred more frequently during the last two years.

'What is the reason?' I asked.

'Curiosity,' Joseph answered.

As usual, nowadays, I knew that my next question would annoy Joseph, but I did not seem to be able to control my tongue.

'Nothing more?' I asked.

'Meaning what?' Joseph enquired.

'Caleb is young,' I said. 'And to have such a success with his preaching I would presume he must be attractive.'

Joseph looked at me calmly. What I had implied did not seem to have irritated him at all.

'Can you not believe that I may have changed during the last two or three years?' he asked.

'Sometimes I can,' I replied. 'I am not sure.'

Joseph sighed. 'Is it possible that you wish I had not altered my ways?' he demanded.

'Life was happier before you became a politician,' I confessed. 'Before you became so strict and virtuous.'

'Life seemed happier – because in those days we were both younger,' Joseph stated.

'Have I aged so much?' I asked him.

'You are still slim and spry and elegant,' Joseph replied. 'I am the one who is no longer young.'

'Were you *ever* young?' I enquired. 'I sometimes wonder.'

Joseph smiled. For an instant he touched his neatly trimmed beard with its streaks of grey.

'Once,' he answered. 'At one time I was young. Long, long ago – centuries back it must surely have been – I seem to remember friends of my parents coming to the house. "So there's little Joseph," they would say. "And how is young Joseph today?" they would ask as they ruffled the curls on my head. So you see, my dear Raguel, in those days I *must* have been young.'

'But did you ever feel young?' I persisted.

'Yes. I can remember one occasion,' Joseph began and then stopped himself. 'But why are you so disturbed this morning, Raguel?' he asked. 'Merely because I have asked a new preacher to come and see me?'

'No.'

'Why then?'

Suddenly I had an instinct which told me the moment had come to tell Joseph the truth about what had been making me unhappy.

'These last few months I have been worried,' I said. 'I have been worried because I feel I may be losing you.'

Joseph stared at me in surprise.

'We live in the same house, here and in Jerusalem,' he reminded me. 'We will be together, I trust, until I die. So how can you be losing me?'

'You are not the same person I met twelve years ago,' I said firmly.

'Nor are you,' Joseph replied. 'Because we all change.'

'How am I different?' I enquired.

Joseph paused. When he spoke I knew he had given himself time to select his phrases carefully.

'I would say you are wiser and more cautious,' he began. 'You are more intelligent and understanding. You are smoother in manner. And you are a far better poet.'

'But I am no longer young.'

'You *look* young.'

'Not to you, Joseph,' I said.

Joseph rose from his chair, crossed the room, and put his hand on my shoulder.

'What have I done to worry you so much?' he asked.

'You have withdrawn into a shell,' I answered. I could hear the tremor in my voice. I no longer had control over the words that came swirling into my mind. 'You are still kind to me,' I told him. 'But then, you try to be kind to everyone to whom you feel yourself indebted. So you are kind to Manasseh because he taught you carpentry and sometimes took your side against your father. You are kind to Leah because you feel guilty about her arm and you can still hear her screams when the oil poured over it. You are kind to Ben because you were once attracted by him. And you are kind to me because you once loved me. But I have no wish to become just another relic of your past.'

Joseph moved away from me and stood, leaning against one of the columns, looking out at the lake.

'Are you angry with me?' he asked quietly. 'Or are you angry with yourself for some reason I do not know about?'

'You should never have given up your study of medicine in your youth,' I told him. 'You would have made a great physician, dissecting people's bodies as dispassionately as you can dissect their minds. You can be kind, Joseph, but you can be harsh sometimes and quite cruel.'

'Is that so odd?' Joseph asked, his back still turned to me.

I now began to feel a little ashamed of the violence of my words. But there was one last thing I had to tell him, and then I would say no more.

'There is a change in you, Joseph, which worries me most of all,' I said. 'You have become secretive.'

Joseph did not speak. He stood motionless, facing the lake. There was a knock at the main door. Joseph glanced around and saw me moving out of the room.

'Let Manasseh go to answer it,' he said quietly. 'It gives him pleasure to feel he is useful.'

'Manasseh is in his shed,' I explained.

'But he always listens for a knock at the door,' Joseph replied.

I pointed to the corner by the window. 'Manasseh has made you another table,' I told him.

When Joseph smiled at me, I knew he had forgiven my outburst.

'Soon we will have to build a new wing to the house to contain them all,' Joseph said.

'Or persaude him to work in the garden,' I suggested.

'Never!' Joseph exclaimed. 'Manasseh is far too proud.'

'Because he taught you carpentry?'

'No,' Joseph replied. 'Because he was a Zealot and a very brave patriot.'

'You say "was a Zealot",' I said. 'But isn't he still one?'

'No,' Joseph answered. 'He promised me some years ago that he would give up being one of their followers.'

'He may have promised you, but I suspect that in practice he has remained one,' I stated. I would have said more but at that moment Manasseh came in from the inner courtyard.

'Good morning, Master Joseph,' Manasseh said.

'I am delighted with the new table,' Joseph told him. 'It is most charming.'

'Good,' Manasseh replied. 'I'm glad you like it, Master.'

Manasseh opened the door that led to the outer courtyard. Once again Joseph smiled at me. We heard a creaking sound as the main door was pulled open, and then the noise of a crowd outside. Above the din we heard Ben's voice.

'Quick, Master,' he was saying. 'Come in.'

'Shut the door after him, stupid,' a second voice – probably Gomer's – cried out.

The babble of the crowd died away as the door was closed.

'This way, Master,' Ben said.

I knew that Caleb was only a few years older than Ben, so I found it ridiculous that Ben should call him 'Master'.

'You go first and show us the way, stupid,' Gomer's voice – by now I was sure it was Gomer – said. 'You know the house, and we don't.'

'All right,' we heard Ben reply.

Suddenly, for some reason, I had a premonition that something disturbing was about to occur. I felt nervous. A moment later, Ben came in followed by Gomer. Then Caleb appeared. And immediately I was aware of the cause of my foreboding. For Caleb looked younger than I had imagined, and he was unusually handsome. Moreover there was a kind of intensity about him which I found alarming. It was as if some form of light emanated from him with a strange brilliance. My instinct was at once antagonistic towards him – perhaps because I was afraid of being overwhelmed by the radiance of his presence. I glanced at Joseph. His face told me nothing. I forced myself to remain detached. I made myself examine Caleb as I would examine any other stranger to the house.

Typically enough, Caleb wore the white robe of a healer. But on to it had been stitched patches of material of different colours. Around his narrow waist was a thick leather belt. From his neck hung a garland of wild flowers. His light-brown hair which fell to his shoulders looked as if it had been oiled and meticulously combed and brushed. His skin was smooth and beardless. His hands looked very soft. Each nail of his fingers had been carefully trimmed. 'Here,' I now thought to myself with a slight surge of optimism, 'here is quite probably an impostor.'

But as I looked at Caleb's face I was not certain that my guess was right, for there was an air of definite integrity in his expression. His eyes which were wide-set and of the same blue as the irises on my balcony contrasted pleasantly with his olive skin and brown hair. Immediately beneath the lower lashes of his eyes were small creases, tiny folds of fat, such as you see in the eyes of a child, which gave him a look of innocence. Indeed, there was a softness about all his features – the small, rather fleshy nose with its over-large nostrils, the broad mouth and full lips, the smooth cheeks, and the slim neck, poised gracefully on his shoulders. There was no doubt that Caleb was an extremely attractive young man. But once again it was the expression of his face and his whole attitude which most fascinated me. Without seeming at all vain or supercilious Caleb appeared to be completely at ease and confident as if he were already certain that Joseph and I would become his friends.

Bustling around Caleb, more squat than ever but with a new air of importance, was Gomer, who gave me a grin of recognition. Caleb raised his hands and put his palms together in salutation, first to Joseph and then to me.

'Peace be with you,' he said in Aramaic. I noticed he spoke

with the faint country burr of the district which I have always liked.

'Welcome,' Joseph replied.

'You already know Ben,' Caleb said to Joseph, 'but I do not think you have met Gomer.'

'No, I have not met him,' Joseph answered.

Gomer waddled forward, gave me a quick nod, and then bowed low in salutation to Joseph.

'We have not met, sir. But I have heard about you, sir,' Gomer said, spitting out his words in his excitement so that flecks of froth appeared on his lips. 'Indeed I have. I've heard of all your generosity to the poor of this village. I know you are greatly respected in Jerusalem – with powerful connections. A trained doctor in medicine as well.'

I looked at Caleb. He was obviously amused by Gomer's effusiveness. He smiled at Joseph. It was quite a charming smile, without any guile or reticence.

'Gomer and I were both impressed when we heard you were a member of the Sanhedrin,' Caleb said to Joseph cheerfully.

Joseph smiled back at him. I could see he was already attracted to the young man but determined not to show it.

'I am afraid that membership of the Sanhedrin is less impressive than it sounds,' Joseph told him. 'In political matters we in the Sanhedrin can only recommend. The man who executes our decisions is the Roman Governor, Valerius Gratus. The Roman Governor is always the final master.'

Joseph spoke to Manasseh who was now standing by the door. 'Can we have some wine for our guests?' he asked. Then he turned back to Caleb. 'Or do you not take wine?' he enquired.

'On occasions,' Caleb replied, as Manasseh left the room. 'Today will be one of them.'

Joseph made a sweeping gesture with his arm. 'Please let us all sit down,' he said.

For a moment Joseph looked at Caleb in silence.

'You are not at all what I expected,' Joseph told his guest.

Caleb laughed. 'Whatever did you expect?' he asked. 'An old man with a wispy grey beard and a bald head? Surely they must have told you I was only young?'

'They did,' Joseph answered. 'But I thought you would look more serious.'

Suddenly the faintly mischievous, rather childlike expression left Caleb's face, and for the first time he appeared solemn.

'I *am* very serious,' he replied quietly.

' "Serious" may not be the correct word I am seeking,' Joseph said. 'I had imagined you would look a trifle grim.'

'Why should I?' Caleb asked. 'Because I preach righteousness?'

'No,' Joseph answered. 'I thought you would look severe, because most of the prophets – or so we are told – have looked wild-eyed and haggard. And I gather you claim to be a prophet.'

'I *am* a prophet,' Caleb answered simply.

By now I sensed that, despite his self-control, Joseph was already beginning to be stirred by the young man's confidence and charm. Most probably, it was in order to disguise his emotions that Joseph now began to address Caleb severely.

'Abraham was our first prophet,' Joseph told him. 'Abraham received a personal and specific summons from God. Has God summoned *you*?'

'Yes,' Caleb replied.

'God has called our Master,' Gomer said. 'Caleb has heard God's voice.'

'The prophetic awareness of history began with Moses,' Joseph continued, ignoring Gomer. 'There were always symbols to be found in the announcement of a prophetic message. There was also an intercessory aspect of the task of a prophet. He would plead to God on behalf of mankind. Lastly, in the personality of each one of the prophets we know there can be discovered a combination of the power to proclaim and the power to predict. Do you have such powers?'

'I believe so,' Caleb answered calmly.

Though Joseph's tone of voice had been stern, I had been interested to observe there was no trace of animosity in Caleb's replies to the questions.

'Caleb's prophetic powers are abundant, sir,' Gomer said to Joseph.

'You are probably aware that there are three reasons for the practice of foretelling the future,' Joseph continued, still ignoring Gomer. 'First, if people are to have any moral responsibility for the present, they must obviously be made aware of the future. Next, since the prophets speak in the name of the Holy Ruler of History, they must know the truth. Moreover, the practice of warning and prediction is very much a part of a prophet's work. Thus in the scriptures we read of the people being warned against their tolerance of Canaanite worship.'

Joseph paused and gazed straight towards Caleb.

'As you may know,' he continued, 'prostitution in those days was given the blessing of the Canaanite priests. Both male and female prostitutes formed a part of the temple staff and lived beside the sanctuaries and shrines. Another thing you should know. Jeremiah tells us that a *false* prophet is a man of immoral ways who does not object to immorality in others. Whereas the *true* prophet tries to stem the tide of evil and to call his people to goodness. And another thing. The message of a false prophet will always be one of peace, irrespective of the moral state of the country. However, the country's moral state is a prerequisite of peace. So the *true* prophet does not preach peace but the sword. He urges men to prepare themselves to fight against evil and to slay their oppressors. Are you aware of these distinctions?'

'I have read the scriptures,' Caleb answered.

Joseph was now looking steadily at Caleb.

'Then what makes you so certain that God has chosen *you*?' he asked.

'To give one reason,' Caleb replied, 'because I have prophetic gifts.'

'He truly has, I promise you,' Ben said eagerly. 'Our Master is a great prophet.'

'He is the best prophet we have ever known in the district,' Gomer added. 'He can tell you your past, your present, and your future.'

'So can the priests of heathen oracles – or so we are informed,' I pointed out.

'But they are all over the place in their reckonings,' Gomer said. 'They hedge their bets. The replies of the oracles of Delphi and of Jupiter Ammon in Egypt are too often evasive and uncertain. But our Master is accurate. He can see straight into a man's mind.' Gomer gave me a leer. 'At times it is quite awkward,' he concluded.

Manasseh came in. He was carrying a jar of wine and cups on a tray. He began to hand round the wine. Joseph spoke softly to Caleb.

'Do you know this man?' he asked.

'I know he works for you,' Caleb replied.

'And Caleb might have heard more than that,' I stated.

'He hasn't,' Ben told us. 'I'm sure of it.'

'Very well,' Joseph said to Caleb. 'Can we test your powers?'

'If you want to,' Caleb answered.

'Then allow me to put my first question,' Joseph said. 'What is the man's name?'

Caleb smiled. Once again I was conscious of his charm. The small crease beneath each of his eyes seemed to grow deeper when he smiled – which for some reason made his face appear even more attractive.

'A prophet does not need to find out a man's name to know about him,' Caleb replied.

'But surely a man's name is part of his character?' I said.

'How many men do you know called Simeon?' Caleb asked. 'Apart from their name what have they in common?'

'Never mind the name,' Joseph said. 'What can you tell us about this man?'

'Let us try,' Caleb murmured, half to himself.

He turned to Manasseh and gave him his usual deferential salutation. 'Peace be with you,' he said.

'And with you,' Manasseh replied, handing him a cup of wine. Then Manasseh looked enquiringly towards Joseph.

'This is Caleb,' Joseph explained to him. 'The preacher we have heard about. He is going to try out his gifts on you. Do not be afraid, and do not interrupt.' Joseph turned back to Caleb. 'Now for my second question. Has the man any particular trade?'

Caleb gazed at Manasseh. I was aware that he was making an intense effort of concentration.

'You are a man of various trades,' he said, speaking very slowly. 'You can mend almost anything that is broken. What is more, you are very good carpenter.'

I noticed that now Caleb was wholly absorbed in Manasseh the burr in his accent had become more pronounced. But from his lips the slightly slurred speech of the district sounded even more pleasant than usual. Caleb moved towards the window and examined the little table I had put in the corner.

'You made this table,' he said to Manasseh. 'You made it well, if I may say so. It is simple, and it is beautiful.'

'Thank you,' Manasseh answered.

'But the whole village knows that Manasseh is a carpenter,' I felt obliged to remind them. 'Everyone knows he is the odd-job man here.'

Caleb smiled at me. 'I am not a liar,' he said gently. 'And I am not a fraud.'

'Can you tell us about Manasseh's past?' Joseph asked him. 'For instance, where was he born?'

'Jezreel,' Caleb replied.

'A bit further north,' said Manasseh whom Caleb had evidently won over to his side by admiring his carpentry.

'You must not help him,' Joseph ordered.

'Shunem,' Caleb said suddenly.

'Right,' Manasseh cried.

'But second time,' I pointed out. Already, I suppose, I was beginning to be jealous of Caleb; already I was envious of his easy confidence and gracious manner.

'But what is the use of my telling the past?' Caleb now asked Joseph.

'We cannot test your powers of prophecy about the future – because we cannot prove that your prophecy is correct,' Joseph told him. 'Over the past, we can do so.'

'Why should you wish to prove me wrong?' Caleb asked.

'I have no such desire,' Joseph replied. 'I want you to convince me that you have at least one of the attributes of a true prophet. So please tell me something about Manasseh's past.'

When Caleb now spoke, it was only the gentleness of his voice and the innocence of the expression on his face which saved his question from sounding insolent.

'Why should I make use of the gifts God gave me for your benefit?' he asked.

'Now, Master,' Gomer said hastily, 'please let us not make any difficulty.'

'*Why* should you use them?' Joseph demanded. 'Because it is always possible that I can help you. Besides, is there anything wrong in using your gifts to prove they are real?'

'Maybe you are right,' Caleb replied. His eyes were fixed on Manasseh, but his words were addressed to Joseph, and he spoke haltingly. 'Manasseh taught you carpentry when you were a small boy,' Caleb began. 'He was a passionate Zealot in those days . . . Today, I would say that he is neither a practising Zealot, nor a Pharisee, nor a Sadducee, nor Essene. But he is a man who prays to God with all his heart.'

35

'Correct but not very startling,' Joseph pronounced.

'And known to several gossips in the village,' I added.

Once again Caleb smiled at me – as if he were amused I so obviously doubted his gifts were genuine. At that moment the new maid, little Merab, came in. She carried a dish of cakes in one hand and a bowl of water in the other. A napkin hung over her left arm, so that as usual in our ritual we could wash our hands before eating food. Though Merab was only seventeen she was pert and confident – probably because she was fully aware how pretty she was. Joseph glanced at her and then turned to me.

'How long has the girl been here?' he asked.

In the old days Joseph would have known the girl's name and all about her. It was typical of his present withdrawn aloofness that he should have been apparently unaware of the girl's presence in the household.

'Nearly a month,' I replied.

Joseph turned back to Caleb. This time when he spoke to him, his voice had lost its tone of severity. 'Can we ask you to try out your gifts on the girl?' he enquired.

'Or do your gifts work only with men?' I could not resist asking, and I looked away from Joseph so that I should not see his frown.

'Can you try?' Joseph repeated.

Caleb nodded his head. Slowly he approached Merab and raised his hands in salutation. 'Peace be with you,' he said softly.

Merab looked up at him for a moment and then handed Caleb the bowl of water. But Caleb did not stretch out his hand, so she offered him a tray of cakes, and he took one. Manasseh had left the room. I poured out more wine for Ben and Gomer.

'What is your name?' Joseph asked the girl.

'Merab,' she replied, glancing at him demurely with her large, dark eyes.

'I want you to answer our guest's questions, Merab,' Joseph told her.

Caleb was now gazing at Merab, contemplating her with a faraway expression on his face, almost as if he were in a trance.

'You come from Jericho,' he said after a while.

Merab shook her head. She turned away from him to Joseph.

'Forgive me, sir,' she murmured, 'but am I allowed to ask what it's all about?'

36

'Our friend claims the gift of insight,' Joseph explained. 'We are testing him. So you must answer his questions, and you must tell us if what he says is true or false.' Joseph addressed Caleb who was standing motionless, watching Merab. 'Please excuse the interruption,' Joseph said. 'Can you proceed, or has the distraction spoiled your concentration?'

Caleb appeared not to have heard Joseph. He took a step towards Merab and began to speak very slowly. 'You are married,' he said. 'You are married to a fisherman . . . On his left shoulder blade your husband has two small scars in the shape of an arrow.'

Merab smiled at Caleb in her demure way. 'You're sure it's the *left* shoulder-blade?' she asked.

'I think so,' Caleb answered. 'Yes,' he continued. 'I can see it now.'

Merab wriggled her shoulders in what I am sure she considered a provocative manner as she looked around the room at the rest of us.

'Well, there may be a fisherman with a mark like that on his shoulder,' she announced, 'but I've never met him, and I'm not married.'

'That's odd,' Caleb muttered to himself.

'I find it odd,' Merab stated, 'but it's the truth.'

I laughed. I looked at Caleb, but he did not seem at all perturbed.

'Of course,' he said almost in a whisper. 'You are not married *yet*. I can understand now. It is clear . . . You come from Samaria . . . From the village of Sechem.'

Merab was silent.

'Do you come from Sechem?' Joseph asked her.

'Yes, sir,' Merab replied rather sulkily.

Caleb was still gazing at her. 'Last night,' he continued, 'late last night you were walking on the hillside. Presently . . . presently you went into some hidden place – a cave perhaps, because it was very dark. You could hardly see. Yes, I am sure it was a cave . . . And there was someone waiting for you. A man was waiting for you . . . You had met this man before – several times.'

While Caleb spoke, I saw that Merab's expression changed. For an instant she gaped at him. Then quickly she controlled herself. But she could not disguise the look of fear which was beginning to invade her face. She was staring at Caleb unwillingly, yet unable to turn away from him.

Caleb now appeared to be deep in his trance and completely unaware of the rest of us in the room. Though I resented the notion, I was beginning to believe his powers of divination might be real.

'I can see the man,' Caleb continued. 'He is a man about thirty years old, lean and dark. And he is very strong . . . Last night this man told you of some plan he had made.'

'Is that true?' Joseph asked Merab.

'No, it is not, sir,' Merab replied quickly. 'There's no truth in it at all. How could there be? I never left the house.'

Caleb did not seem to hear the girl's denial. He spoke very slowly and more hesitantly than before.

'I can see a jackal, lurking outside the cave,' he said. 'You gave – you gave the man something made of silver . . . His name . . . the man's name, I think, was Ephron.'

When Caleb spoke of something silver and then mentioned the name of Ephron, the two disparate fragments of information joined together in my mind, and I could guess what had happened. And this made me aware – once and for all – that however much of a fraud Caleb might be in other respects, his gift of intuition was certainly a genuine one. I glanced towards Joseph, because although he knew nothing of the missing silver plate he must surely remember the name of Ephron, the young man whom we had once employed as a gardener. But Joseph did not appear to have perceived the significance of the name. He was watching Caleb with the air of a father who is disappointed his son has been unable to answer a question put to him in school. I could have interrupted at that moment to tell him I was convinced that Caleb had divined correctly, or I could have given Joseph a nod of confirmation. But I wanted to see how matters would turn out between Joseph and Caleb before I committed myself.

'Then, while you were still in the darkness of the cave, the two of you made a plan together,' Caleb continued. He moved a little closer to the girl. 'Show me your hands,' he ordered.

Nervously, Merab stretched out her hands. I could see her fingers quivering. Caleb moved still closer to her. He now spoke with complete confidence.

'You are wearing no ring,' Caleb said. 'Yet there is something made of metal touching your skin at this moment . . . Yes, it is metal . . . There is something gold. You are touching something gold.'

When he spoke the word 'gold' Caleb's trance seemed to leave him, and his features became less taut. He stood silently watching Merab.

Suddenly he must have become aware of the look of fear in the girl's eyes. He had begun to speak again, but he stopped himself. He smiled at Merab very gently.

'Something you were lent, one would suppose,' Caleb said. 'Something you will in time return.'

'Can that be true, Merab?' Joseph asked.

Merab glanced towards Caleb who was smiling at her encouragingly. For an instant the girl hesitated, then she turned back to Joseph. 'Of course not, sir,' she answered.

Joseph addressed Caleb. 'Do you want to try again?' he asked.

Caleb was still watching Merab. 'No,' he answered quietly.

'If you will forgive me, sir,' the girl said to Joseph. 'I'll be going. Leah's out at the market, and cook needs me in the kitchen.'

'You can go,' Joseph told her, and Merab moved towards the door leading to the back courtyard.

'So on this last occasion your intuition failed you, Caleb,' Joseph said.

At that instant Merab came to a halt. Slowly she turned round. She was gaping in astonishment.

'Caleb?' Merab asked in an awed voice. 'The Caleb they talk about? Caleb the preacher?'

'Yes, indeed,' Gomer replied unctuously.

'I didn't know,' the girl said to Caleb. 'Please forgive me.'

'I have nothing to forgive,' Caleb replied. 'You must ask God to forgive any wrong you may have done.'

Merab nodded her head. Her large eyes were staring at Caleb beseechingly.

'I promise,' she murmured. 'And I am sorry.'

By now Caleb seemed to have shaken off the effects of his trance completely. He appeared once again young and lighthearted.

'God will certainly bless you,' he told Merab cheerfully.

'Thank you,' the girl said. 'Thank you, Master.' And she hurried out of the room.

Joseph looked disapprovingly at Caleb. 'By what right do you tell the girl that God will bless her?' he asked. 'I cannot believe that you presume to speak in God's name?'

'Certainly, I do,' Caleb replied. 'For God speaks through me.'

Caleb spoke so simply and with such conviction that the frown left Joseph's face.

'Be careful, Caleb,' he warned. 'Do not let them hear words like that in Jerusalem.' Then he turned to me. 'Surely Leah would have told one of us if the girl had been out all night?'

'If she had known of it,' I replied without hesitation, 'certainly she would have told us.'

Joseph smiled at Caleb. 'So we may presume that your prophetic gifts are not always accurate,' he declared.

Caleb laughed. 'No, they are not,' he answered. 'For instance, I was wrong about Merab's marriage. I believed I was seeing the past, when in fact I was seeing the future.'

'You mean that one day Merab will marry a fisherman with two scars in the shape of an arrow on his left shoulder?' I asked.

'Without any doubt,' Caleb replied.

I handed the dish of cakes round the room. As Caleb put out his hand and took one, his robe fell aside so that we could see the whole length of his right arm. The skin looked very soft. I glanced at Joseph. He was staring at Caleb's arm. Suddenly I knew by instinct what was in Joseph's mind. He was thinking, as I had been, that the skin of the whole of Caleb's body must be as soft as the skin of his arm. And as I watched Joseph, I knew that in his mind he was taking off Caleb's robe and imagining him completely naked as he had once imagined me as I sat on the roof of his house in Jerusalem.

'How long are you staying on this side of the lake?' I asked Caleb.

'I am not certain,' Caleb replied. 'I am seldom certain what I will do next. I expect I shall stay here a few more weeks. I hope we shall meet again.'

'Certainly,' Joseph replied in a polite but casual tone of voice. 'I hope so too. I would like to have a talk with you. Would you care to come to see me tomorrow?'

Suddenly Ben rose to his feet. 'You can talk now if you want,' he announced. 'Gomer and I have to go back to the village for a while.'

'Gomer gulped down his wine. 'Quite right, Ben,' he said. 'Quite right.'

'We'll wait for you in the market,' Ben told Caleb. Then he gave a small wave of his hand to Joseph and to me and grinned at us happily. 'Thank you for the wine,' he said.

'And the cakes,' Gomer added. 'Thank you very much.' Then he made a bow to Joseph and nodded to me, and left the room followed by Ben.

For a while there was silence. Joseph glanced towards me to see if I intended to leave him alone with Caleb, but I pretended to be looking in another direction. I was still uncertain what I should do, for I did not know how the situation was going to develop. But as I looked at young Caleb with his cheerful and childlike face, his lovely eyes and shining hair, his smooth olive skin, and his slender body, I was conscious that for the first time since I had met Joseph I was confronted with an acute threat to our companionship. I could appreciate the power of Caleb's charm because, of course, I was drawn to him myself. If I had not loved Joseph so strongly I could easily imagine myself becoming passionately fond of Caleb. I may seem to be over-generous in my assessment of him, but I could not help being entranced by the signs which his whole being and his every movement seemed to proclaim that he was passionate and sensual. His presence exuded a strange animal quality, yet he was without doubt sincere in his beliefs. Moreover we are told we should never underestimate our enemy. And Caleb was my enemy, for I was afraid he would attract Joseph not only by his charm, but by his enthusiasm and intelligence. Perhaps he would do so unwillingly. Yet what did I know of Caleb's motives? He might need money to support his followers and to extend the area of his influence. Or he might have more personal motives for needing money. How could I tell? I could only wait and watch what would happen, and control events if I was able to. There was a further danger. I was afraid of Caleb's power of intuition. How far did it extend? Could he read my mind as he sat facing Joseph, glancing at at me from time to time?

I poured out more wine into our cups.

'Where will you go when you leave Galilee?' Joseph asked Caleb.

'Perhaps to Samaria,' Caleb replied. 'Perhaps to Jerusalem.'

Joseph seemed thoughtful. 'From what I have heard of your teaching, I would suppose you would have more success in the villages than the towns,' Joseph said after a pause. 'Therefore, please may I advise you to stay in the countryside, here in the north.'

Caleb was silent.

'In a way we are fortunate to be in Galilee,' Joseph continued. 'We are surrounded by pagan districts. Plenty of foreigners – both Greeks and Syrians – live around us. The whole of Samaria separates us from the strict centre of our religion. There is no sympathy here for the strenuous legalism of the Pharisees in Jerusalem. So if you wish your preaching to succeed, let me advise you to stay in these parts and avoid the towns.'

'Perhaps success is not quite what Caleb wants,' I murmured.

'What do you hope to accomplish?' Joseph asked him.

'What God intends me to,' Caleb answered. 'It is not all of it clear to me yet. But God has told me that I must prepare the ground.'

Caleb now started to speak more urgently. His voice began to ring with excitement. 'I am certain of one thing,' he continued, his face glowing with a childlike eagerness. 'I know that the greatest moment of our age is very near. We of this very generation will experience the coming of the Kingdom of God on earth. And there is not much time, so we must get ready now. All mankind must be prepared to place itself at God's will. Every single one of us must be ready to abandon his family and friends – to leave behind every possession. We must be prepared to break all earthly relationships in order to obey God's call.'

Caleb paused. His eyes seemed to have grown very large.

'Try to understand, both of you,' he cried. 'The greatest event the world has ever seen is going to take place in our lifetime – the most wonderful happening mankind has ever witnessed. And can you possibly advise me to limit *that* message to country villages?'

Joseph spoke in a flat, deliberately calm voice. 'Yes,' he said, 'I do thus advise you.'

'Are you unable to understand?' Caleb demanded with a kind of bewildered innocence. 'I must tell everyone I can find. I must make them listen to me. All prophecy is going to be fulfilled while we are still alive. The end of Israel's suffering is imminent – the end of all history. We shall see the final struggle between the followers of light and darkness, between God and the forces of evil. All of us – whether we wish it or not – will be involved in that holy war, here on earth. It will be very soon now. And the words of the prophet Isaiah will come true. A new Teacher of Righteousness will appear. He will be the Messiah, the Son of the Living God. And a new Israel will rise out of the fire of the nation's misery. For the Messiah will redeem Israel. He will establish divine rule on earth. The Son of God will come, I tell you. Perhaps he has been born already. He may be living among us, waiting for the sign.'

Caleb raised his head. I felt he was no longer addressing us directly, for he had withdrawn into some private vision of his own which seemed to transform his face with joy.

'Even more wonderful,' Caleb continued, speaking almost to himself, 'the happiness of his salvation will be shared by Jew and Gentile alike. God will bless not only the poor and suffering but the outcasts and misfits of the world. He will bless the lame in spirit and the deformed in mind. Above all, he will bless the humble, and he will bless the sinners – for God is very near to them and calls them to himself.'

Joseph spoke very quietly. 'I can understand what you are saying,' he told Caleb. 'I personally sympathize with your message. But you must remember that throughout Palestine today there is an increasing hysteria. Many people have come to expect the Messiah almost hourly. But I must warn you that you are not the kind of prophet they are expecting to herald the Messiah's arrival. Far from it. You are too young. Besides, if I may say so, despite your enthusiasm, you are too simple at heart to confound the priests in Jerusalem.' Joseph gave Caleb a warm smile. 'Lastly,' he said, 'I must tell you, as I have told you before, that your appearance is not one of a prophet. I believe you could make a fine leader of a large number of country people. I do not see you as a prophet.'

'Yet I *am* a prophet,' Caleb replied firmly. 'And God has ordered me to prophesy. He has instructed me to spread the good news.'

'Do you seriously think they would ever listen to you in Jerusalem?' Joseph asked.

'Yes – if God so wills,' Caleb answered.

'You would arouse hostility from the Pharisees and Sadducees,' Joseph told him. 'I am sure that Raguel agrees with me. You would be thrown out within a week.'

'He might be,' I replied cautiously.

'Raguel, you know he would,' Joseph stated. 'First, they would throw him out of the temple, and then they would chase him out of Jerusalem.'

'Why should people believe a band of Pharisees and Sadducees more than they believe me?' Caleb demanded. 'The Sadducees only draw their strength from the priestly classes and the so-called nobility. Sadducees! They are so conservative and narrow-minded, they have persuaded themselves to believe that the only way to reach God lies up some weird ladder of knowledge they have created in their own

43

devious minds. They believe that simple uneducated people will never find God. But I tell you that the poor and simple will find God sooner than the learned Sadducees or any of the Scribes in Jerusalem.'

Caleb paused. In his indignation he looked like a boy who has been unjustly accused of a fault by his master. 'And why should people listen to the Pharisees?' he asked. 'Pharisees! Punctilious, earnest and devout – I grant them that. But can they honestly believe that our future as the holy people of God consists in keeping the law down to the smallest detail? From the moment a Pharisee awakes in the morning to the moment he goes to sleep at night, all he can think about is ritual piety. Should the towel he uses for drying his hands be placed on a table or a cushion? Should the evening prayer be made standing up or lying in bed? Is it lawful to eat an egg that is laid on the Sabbath – or an egg that is formed inside the hen on that day and laid on the next? The Pharisees must either be fools or hypocrites – with their idiotic, petty little observances and pedantry.'

'No,' Joseph interrupted suddenly. 'You must not say such things in my house. You must at least be fair. My father was a Pharisee, and for all his failings he was a patriotic and religious man. He tried with all his might to preserve the traditions and customs of our country from the contamination of a foreign power. Never forget that, unlike the Sadducees who are inclined to collaborate with the Romans, the Pharisees strive to preserve our nation intact.'

'But surely they go the wrong way about it?' Caleb asked, unperturbed by Joseph's interruption. 'I tell you this. God is a spirit, and he must be worshipped in spirit. I am here to preach that message. Cannot you see? I am here to preach the tidings that eternal happiness is close to us. Eternal happiness and eternal life. I am the bearer of wonderful news. Therefore I cannot limit my message. I must go to Jerusalem so that my message can spread.'

'Not yet,' Joseph told him. 'Do not take the risk yet. Let your news spread gradually. Make sure of your following, and you will become a power the priests and councillors in Jerusalem will be unable to dispose of easily.'

'I believe Caleb is powerful already,' I said.

Joseph glanced at me in surprise.

'Only in parts of Galilee,' he replied.

I rose from my chair. 'Caleb has power,' I said as I moved towards the door leading to the inner courtyard. 'I only wonder if it will turn out to be a power for good.'

I smiled at Joseph. 'I will be in my room should you need me,' I told him. I nodded pleasantly and politely to Caleb. 'I look forward to hearing you preach,' I said. 'I am sure it is quite an experience.' Then I left the room.

I had spoken ambiguously because I did not want either of them as yet to be certain of the turn of my mind or of my general attitude. But already I had devised a plan of sorts.

However, at that moment, I could not tell how it would work out.

CHAPTER TWO

I must admit I was glad when Raguel left the room, for his presence was imposing a strain on me. I am very much afraid that Raguel thinks I invited Caleb to the house only because I had heard he was good-looking, and I fear that Raguel is now suffering from his usual pathetic jealousy. I say 'pathetic', for he has really no cause to be jealous at all. It is true – I certainly confess it to myself – it is true that I am no longer in love with Raguel. But I will never be in love with anyone else and, as I tried to tell him just now, I value him greatly as a friend, and I hope he will stay with me until I die. Of course Caleb is attractive – very much so. Of course I enjoy admiring his high-spirited enthusiasm and his wonderfully graceful body. Perhaps he is the most attractive young man I have ever met. But even this admission to myself cannot deflect me from my task.

It is a sad thing that I am pledged not to reveal my secret to Raguel. My friends in the organization have forbidden it. They say that to tell him would be an unnecessary risk. I have argued against them in vain. I am beginning to suspect they do not trust Raguel. I know they are aware that he has fits of jealousy. What they cannot appreciate is his complete loyalty to me.

As my mind returned to the living-room, I suddenly became conscious that Caleb had spoken.

'Forgive me,' I said. 'My mind was far away. It is a bad habit I have.'

'Please do not think me impertinent,' Caleb said. 'But may I ask you a question?'

'Certainly,' I answered.

'Why is Raguel sad?' Caleb asked.

'I was under the impression that you could tell everyone's thoughts,' I murmured.

'Not when there is a veil between us,' Caleb replied.

I gazed at Caleb in silence. He watched me calmly.

'I think you will discover the answer to your question one of these days,' I told Caleb. 'It is not for me to give it you.'

'I like Raguel,' Caleb said. 'But he has an odd quality of despair. I wish I could help him.'

Without any volition on my part, I began to think once again about Raguel. And I remembered him as a boy, his face a little flushed, leaning forward as he sat on the couch on my roof, his eyes gleaming, the words stumbling one after the other, as he told me in excited phrases of his ambition to become a poet. What exactly has *happened* to Raguel over the years? I am not sure.

I must have spoken the last sentence aloud, for I suddenly saw Caleb smiling at me. 'What are you not sure about?' he asked.

'I thought you could read my mind,' I said.

'Not at the moment,' Caleb replied.

'Can you read my past?' I enquired.

At that instant Caleb and I looked at each other. For a while we were silent. I was conscious that this was the first time we had been alone together. I was very much aware of his presence in the room as he sat quietly on his chair, close to me. Suddenly I felt I had been friends with him for a long time. I felt I knew the workings of his brain. And I knew each fold and muscle of his body, for I could now imagine I had made love to him.

'So you are still wondering if I have true prophetic gifts?' Caleb asked.

'I would like to think so,' I answered.

'You do not believe I can tell the past?'

'Not yet.'

Caleb pointed to the gold signet ring I wore on my right hand. 'Have you worn that ring for some time?' he enquired.

'My father died over twenty years ago,' I told him. 'I have worn the ring since then.'

'Can I hold it for a moment?' Caleb asked.

I handed him the ring. As Caleb took it from me, I noticed that he was very careful not to touch my fingers. I wondered what contamination it could be that he feared. He held the ring between the palms of his hands.

'Your father was a rich man,' Caleb began slowly. 'He made a fortune organizing a safe camel-route for traders . . . They were protected from robbers all the way from Jerusalem to Alexandria.'

'True,' I admitted. 'But, as you will appreciate, fairly common knowledge.'

'Your father limped,' Caleb told me. 'He was sometimes unkind to your mother . . . There was a woman he had met after his marriage whom he loved . . . He was often violent . . . Towards the end of his life, he was sometimes mad.'

Between each of Claeb's phrases there came a pause lasting so long that I would think he had nothing more to say. But then he would begin to speak once again. All that he had said – so far – about my father was accurate.

'Your father was very severe with you,' Caleb continued. 'He was a strict Pharisee – but you told me that already. However, I do not think you told me that at the age of twelve you were sent to a school in Jerusalem.'

Once again Caleb paused. These silences of his, I decided, were one of his oddest mannerisms. During them he seemed wholly withdrawn. He looked very young and a little dazed.

'Can you tell me something that only I could know?' I asked.

Caleb began playing with the signet ring, now turning it over between the palms of his hands, now holding it in one hand and stroking it with the fingers of the other. Suddenly he stopped. With a quick gesture he put down the ring on to the table between us as if the metal had been burning him. He looked distraught. For a while he hesitated. Then he began to speak in a quiet voice.

'Two years later, during the holidays, you left Jerusalem,' he continued. 'You took a school friend with you to stay at your father's house in the country. By then your mother had died, but your father had not married again . . . One night your father went into the town for a meeting of the local council – or so you thought . . . But he returned an hour later. He came back very quietly. So you did not hear him . . . He opened the door of your room. When he found –

47

when he found what he had been afraid to find, he sent your friend away from the house, ordering a servant to escort the boy back to Jerusalem. Then your father made you come to his own room . . . And he whipped you. He whipped you till you bled.'

Caleb's voice had dropped to a whisper. The room was so silent that I could hear the creak of the oars of a boat, close on the lake outside, and the faint splashing of the water.

'So you know why he whipped me?' I asked.

Caleb did not answer. I doubt if he had heard what I said.

'Are you shocked?' I asked.

Caleb was still silent, but I had an instinct that he had been more disturbed by the thought of my father's violence than by what I had done. In fact, surprisingly enough, I felt a warm sympathy flowing from Caleb towards me. I was now certain that he liked me, and – far more important – that he had confidence in me.

'They tell me you prefer to live alone,' I said. 'Has desire of some kind never tempted you?'

'Of course it has,' Caleb answered.

'But you resisted?' I enquired. 'You overcame it?'

The solemnity left Caleb's face, and he laughed. He picked up the ring and gave it back to me. Once again I observed that he was careful not to touch my hand.

'I never intended to give that impression,' he told me.

As he smiled at me, with a shock I sensed that for all the gentleness of his appearance there was a strong virility about Caleb. I felt that his body was capable of intense passion. I suppose this was one of the reasons I had been attracted to him as soon as we had met.

'When I was sixteen there was a girl in the village where I lived, a few miles above the town of Cana,' Caleb explained. 'The girl was a year older than I was. Her name was Sarah, and she was very lovely. And I wanted her. I needed her. I thought about her night after night in my bed. Sometimes in my mind I had her. Only in my mind. But I believed that what I was doing was a sin. So I decided I must forget about her. That was my decision.'

Caleb had spoken his last words defiantly – as if he felt that I would disapprove of his reasoning.

'Several days passed by,' Caleb continued. 'Then, one evening, I was wandering at the far end of the vineyard that belonged to my father, and I met the girl again. And all my resolve was swept away by the force of my desire for the girl. We stood in silence, watching each other. I was trembling. I could not move. I could not speak. The girl was staring at me. I suppose the expression of my face told her the troubles of my mind. Anyhow, suddenly she turned and walked away. I wanted to follow her. I wanted to seize her and hold her in my arms. But my fear kept me rooted to the ground. And later, when I was about to move, I saw her going back into her parents' house.'

'Nothing more?' I asked.

'Nothing,' Caleb answered.

'And in the years since then?'

'I have been able to suppress desire,' Caleb told me. 'You see, I found I had to. Just as wine blurs the senses, so I found that desire blurred my communion with God.'

'How did you manage to overcome desire?' I asked.

'God helped me,' Caleb answered. 'He gave me a fear just as strong as my temptation – stronger perhaps.'

'What fear?'

For a while Caleb did not reply. He was gazing down at his almost full cup of wine on the table.

'I have an intense fear of being touched,' he answered after a pause. 'I am afraid of any contact. That is the reason I ask my disciples to keep the crowds away from me. I cannot bear someone brushing against me. That is why, although I can sometimes cure the sickness of a man's mind, I cannot heal his body, for I cannot touch it. I am unable to take his hand, so my force cannot run through his body to cure him.'

'Do you really believe that if you touched a leper you would cure his leprosy?' I asked.

'Yes – if he believed in me.'

'How long ago did you leave home?'

'When I was seventeen.'

'Why?' I asked. 'Were you unhappy?'

Caleb looked up from contemplating his cup. His eyes seemed to be searching my face as if needed to discover the answer to some question. The result of his examination must have satisfied him because he nodded his head. And when he now began to speak I had the impression he intended to tell me of events which he had confided only to few people – if, indeed, to anyone.

'I spent part of my time at school, and part of my time working in the vineyard,' he began. 'As I told you, my father had a vineyard in the terraces of land far above Cana. He was a good man. But sometimes he drank too much of his own wine, and then he would rave about anything that came into his head. Usually it was about the stock from which he was sprung. He claimed that he was descended from King David and that in his veins flowed royal blood. My mother would listen to him patiently, and after a while we would help him to bed. I loved my mother very much. Her kindness never seemed to fail her. In those days I was quite contented in a way. I was quite happy in the village school. We had good teachers, and we learned to love the scriptures. I had made friends. I enjoyed life. In fact, I should have been completely happy.'

Caleb paused. I noticed that the strangely withdrawn look was coming back to his face.

'But sometimes I would suffer from a terrible sadness,' he said. 'Even now, I find it hard to describe. I would believe I was missing something. I would feel like a starving man must feel when he looks through an open window into a house at night and sees there is a banquet in progress. Sometimes I felt that I myself was gazing into such a house. I could see the huge, brightly-lit room. I could even see all the guests. But I was always standing alone in the darkness outside, and I was cold and hungry. Then, for days on end, I would be so restless that I would leave my home and school – even though I knew I would be punished for it – and I would wander up into the hills, trying to find out why I was so wretched, why I felt I was missing something. And so the days and months of my boyhood passed by . . . Then, one evening, when I was alone in the hills, suddenly it came – the greatest moment of my life . . . Suddenly, I could see light everywhere – radiant, warm, almost blinding light . . . The light was so intense that I was dazed. For an instant I closed my eyes . . . I was afraid, yet some voice told me there was nothing to fear. And when I opened my eyes, there was still the marvellous light, shining all around me. And suddenly I found I was now inside the vast, brightly-lit room. I was now sitting among the guests at the long gleaming table.'

Caleb raised his head. I knew that he was re-living the moment, for his eyes were enlarged in wonderment.

'Then I knew a happiness so intense it filled all my being,' he continued. 'I turned my eyes towards the direction which all the guests were looking. At the head of the table was an empty chair. The chair was plain. But even though the room was bright, around that chair there was a radiance. Each grain of wood sparkled like gold. And from far away we heard a voice speaking. "One of you will be chosen," the voice said. "One of you will be the elect. For my kingdom – the Kingdom of God – is very near, and all who believe in me will be accepted at my table. Let all know that the Kingdom of God on earth is close. Let them rejoice." Then the voice was silent, and I gazed in bewilderment round the table. And as I stared at the other guests, I found that in some way I could recognize one or two of them. The lean, gaunt-faced man with glowing eyes. The burly man with red cheeks and thick golden hair. The tall man with a raven on his shoulder. And as I tried to distinguish others – other prophets in the assembly – we heard the voice once again. "You who are seated at my table must indeed rejoice," the voice said. "For one of you will be chosen. One of you will be chosen to be the host to all mankind." Then, slowly, the radiance faded, and I was standing on the hillside in the darkness and cold . . . But I was no longer alone. For I knew that God was with me.'

Caleb lowered his head and gazed at me.

'I knew then – that very night – I could never go back home again,' he said. 'I could never listen to the women's gossip and the stories my father told when he had drunk too much wine. At dawn I began to walk. I travelled south. I wandered into the desert. I managed to exist. The nomads were very kind to me, and sometimes I would come across a palm tree with dates clustered on it or a fig tree or sometimes wild honey. One day, however, when I was near to starving, I came to a community of Essenes. They welcomed me and gave me food and drink. Later, one of their Elders told me about their community – how they had given up the pleasure of the senses, considering it a vice. And he explained how the Essenes train themselves in temperance and self-control; how they will not marry, but will adopt other men's children so that the community will not die out; how they have denounced wealth, eat simply and have only one robe; how they till the soil and devote themselves to the world of the spirit. I listened to him carefully. At that time I liked the ideas the Elder had propounded. And the Essenes in that group seemed to like me. So I lived with them for three years.'

'But you left them,' I said. 'Why did you leave the Essenes?'

'Because they are too anxious,' Caleb replied. 'They care too much about orders of precedence and grades of seniority. Everyone has to be junior to someone else. Everybody has to take orders from a senior.'

'Do you object to that?' I asked.

'Yes,' Caleb answered. 'Their idea is wrong because they carry it to absurdity. For instance, if a senior member is touched by a junior one, he must take a bath as if he had been in contact with a heathen. Another thing. The Essenes are all of them ascetics. But I believe we should enjoy the beautiful things of life if we can. The trouble with the Essenes is they are too religious. They spend too much time in rituals and endless discussions. I like them, of course. They are kind. They believe in the brotherhood of man so they do not own slaves. They share everything – money, clothes and food. They are very brave. But they do not enjoy living enough. However, I was fortunate to be with them, for at least I had teachers who could instruct me further in Hebrew. As you have noticed, when I speak Aramaic, I speak with the accent of this part of Galilee. Yet when, as now, I speak Hebrew my accent is less imperfect. But far more important – the Essene teachers had knowledge of every word that had been foretold in various scriptures about the Messiah – how he will go to Jerusalem and preach and be arrested and crucified, how he will suffer and die, but will rise again from death on the third day.'

I was more interested in the customs of the Essenes than in their knowledge of the scriptures.

'Do you believe in sharing money?' I asked Caleb.

'But of course I do,' he answered. 'The little money I have ever had I have given away. I possess no clothes apart from the robes I am wearing. Today, for instance, I have only had a little bread – apart from the cakes you gave me.'

I thought Caleb's reply was specious. His talk about having no money annoyed me. It might be true that Caleb personally had no money. But amongst his followers I knew that Gomer was the treasurer, and I had heard rumours that their funds were quite substantial.

'But you have a father who owns a vineyard,' I reminded Caleb. 'If you were starving, you could always return to the slopes above Cana.'

'My father may be dead for all I know,' Caleb answered. 'And so may my mother.'

'Cana is only a day's journey from here,' I said. 'Surely you would have heard?'

'I doubt it,' Caleb replied. 'When I left home I decided I would never return. That was nearly five years ago. I have not visited the town or the vineyard in the hills since that day.'

'Why not?' I asked.

Caleb sighed. For the first time his face looked sad.

'Sometimes I long to go back,' Caleb answered. 'I would love to see my mother and my father again if they are still alive. But I know that I must not be bound by any bond of love or family affection. No man can follow his inner light until he is freed from the restrictions of family ties. And I must be completely free to serve God.'

'But surely you would have heard if your father had died?'

'No one in this district even knows my father's name,' Caleb replied. 'So how could I have news of him?'

'Were you the only son?' I asked.

'No, I have an elder brother who I suppose is alive.'

'And if you went back to the vineyard, do you think he would deny you a share of it?'

Caleb was silent. He was frowning as if he were trying to work out the solution of a puzzle.

'You are not poor,' I continued. 'So why try to deceive yourself? You do not belong to the same class as peasants and labourers, for your father was a man of means.'

'In the Kingdom of God,' Caleb answered, 'neither wealth nor class will be of any consequence.'

'You may well be right,' I replied. 'But God's Kingdom has not yet come.'

'Not yet. But it will come soon I promise you,' Caleb answered. 'And it is my mission to prepare for that great moment. Meanwhile I must disregard any differences of wealth or class. I must devote myself to spreading my tidings to everyone who will listen to me'. Caleb laughed. 'I suppose you could say I am the hunter who must dig out all people from the burrows of smugness in which they have lived until now,' he added.

I decided that the time had come for me to approach the task which I had been given.

'If there were ever a revolt,' I said, 'a widespread insurrection against the power that oppresses us – would the Essenes fight?'

'Fight the Romans? Yes, I think so,' Caleb replied. 'At least some of them would.'

By now I was convinced I could trust Caleb. There was something about his presence which proclaimed honesty and demanded confidence.

'You believe in promises made before God,' I said.

'Of course I do.'

'Most solemnly?'

'Yes.'

'Do you promise me before God to keep secret every word I now say?' I asked Caleb.

'Before God,' he replied. 'I promise.'

'Then listen to me, Caleb,' I said. 'We both believe that the God of Israel will visit his people to purge the earth of evil. We both believe that what God said of old he will bring to pass. The Messiah, you say, may be with us already. Various prophets have foreseen the time when the Kingdom of God shall be realized. Daniel foresaw the day when Israel would rule over the whole world – the Jews of Israel, not a horde of Roman oppressors. But by choosing us, God has imposed a duty on us. Our duty is to make sure we are ready to receive the Messiah. Yet how can we receive the Messiah, when the land we live in is a mere Roman province – when Roman soldiers strut outside our very temple?'

'If God could deliver us from Egypt,' Caleb said, 'he can deliver us from the Romans.'

'He can,' I agreed, 'but first we must show God that we can help ourselves.'

Caleb was silent. His face was expressionless. The moment had come for me to reveal our plan to him. For some reason I felt nervous.

'Until now, our revolts have failed because they have been mistimed and mismanaged,' I told him. 'But at last a more efficient organization has come into existence. Next time there will be no mistakes. The uprisings will be spontaneous – throughout the countryside and in all the big towns. The Romans will be taken by surprise, and our insurrection will have achieved its victory before they can bring up any reinforcements.'

I was watching Caleb's face carefully. I was uncertain how he would receive the information I had given him. His eyes, which seemed of a startling light blue against the darkness of his hair, were watching me steadily.

'What you have just said surprises me,' Caleb said after a pause. 'I sensed there was a burden on your mind. I could not perceive its nature. Besides, I always thought of you as being well disposed towards the Romans. After all, you are known to have several Roman friends.'

'That does not blind me to the evil of their oppression,' I answered. 'Until our organization is ready there is little we can do. We can be friendly with the Romans if we please. At least it helps to avoid their suspicion. Moreover, we must pay the Romans our taxes in order to exist. And we must obey them. But in our hearts we must obey God. We must get ready to fight for our independence.'

I rose and walked over to Caleb.

'If you will forgive me for saying so, you are young and inexperienced,' I told him. 'But you have great enthusiasm and integrity, and you have a following in Galilee. That is why I received instructions to meet you and to make my own judgment about you. If I did not trust you, I was to say nothing. If I *did* trust you, I was to explain to you the part you could take in our plan. Well, Caleb, I do trust you – completely. So I can tell you exactly how you can help us. It is quite simple. With the training we can give you, then, when the day of the revolt comes, you could lead the insurrection in this district.'

'When that day comes the Romans should be pitied,' Caleb answered, gazing at me solemnly. 'For they will be standing outside in cold darkness, staring enviously into the warm, brightly-lit rooms in which the believers will be assembled. We should be sorry for them, I tell you. Why do you hate them so much?'

'Why? Because beneath their smooth manners they are arrogant and cruel,' I replied. 'Because Jerusalem echoes with the shrieks of men in torture who have been crucified.'

I could see that my answer had not made any impression on Caleb. I was determined not to allow his compassion for the Romans to blind him to their cruelty.

'Have you ever been to the hill?' I asked him.

'No,' Caleb answered. 'Never.'

'I first saw the hill when I was a child,' I began. 'It was my father who took me there.'

I had decided to explain to Caleb the truth of all that had happened, because I wanted him to understand the evil that existed within the boundaries of our land, inside our very country. My words were intended to gain Caleb and his followers as supporters to our side. But as I began speaking I forgot my intention, for my mind had swung back into the past, yet I continued to speak since I found it eased my pain of mind to do so.

I first saw the hill when I was a child, I began.

I was ten years old, I told Caleb, when my father took on a young man called Simon to work in the garden of his house in the country. Simon was about eighteen – very strong and lean, with russet hair and milk-white skin which never seemed to turn brown in the sun. His face was broad, and he looked over-solemn except when he smiled. Simon was a burly man, but his hands when they touched the leaves of a plant were very gentle. I loved the garden with its roses and jasmine, with its gladiolus and narcissus; I could spend hours staring at the scarlet blossoms of the pomegranate and the pink and white blossoms of our almond trees. Sycamore, oak trees and shrubs of tamarisk stood beside acacias and fig trees. Willows drooped over a stream that ran through the end of the garden. And by this stream I would see all kinds of birds – swallows and swifts in their season, doves and cranes, and sometimes white storks, quails and ravens; and Simon would tell me all he knew about them. He was very patient with me.

By now, as I spoke to Caleb, my mind was completely fixed on the past. I could see the local village with its jumble of dun-coloured little houses and flat roof-tops. I could see our house, solid and old-fashioned, set on the slopes above; I could see the outer court with its fountain, and behind it the second court with its surrounding rooms. Inside, I could see the chests with their beautiful ivory inlays, and the gold and silver ornaments on the long wooden table, and the high bed in my own room from which I could look down at the garden below that was green throughout the year because the gardeners watered it at dawn and at dusk in the months of heat.

One morning, while I was idly searching through a clump of white broom, quite close to the stream, I found a dove with a broken leg. The bird was quivering with fear when I picked it up. But Simon with his quiet voice and careful hands soon calmed the dove's trembling. He made a splint for the leg, and presently the dove was eating grain from his hand. I suppose it was then that I first knew I loved Simon.

Some weeks afterwards Simon was given a holiday. He decided to go to Jerusalem. Exactly what occurred during Simon's holiday in Jerusalem has never been found out. But it seems that one evening he was taken to a secret Zealot meeting in the outskirts of the town. The preacher was a fanatic who told his audience that the presence of the Romans in the city was a direct and constant insult to God. He told them it was their duty to destroy the emblems of their heathen oppressors. After the meeting Simon went out and got drunk – or so it was said. What is known for certain is that Simon climbed a high wall and pulled away the bronze eagle on top of a government building. As he climbed down and the crowds roared their approval, some men from a centurion's troop caught him. Simon was imprisoned.

When my father heard the news, he tried to get Simon released. But it was a political offence, and it had been committed in public. The Roman Governor – or Procurator, as the Romans call him – can sentence a man to be crucified not only for mutiny or robbery, but also for any form of rebellion or treachery. Nothing my father could do had any effect. Simon was crucified.

My father was already strange in his moods. The days of his madness were approaching. He now decided to take me to Jerusalem. At noon the following day he made me walk with him up the hill. Each step we took was a penance to me, for I dreaded what we would find there. As we approached I could hear the screams and groans of men in torture. When we reached the top of the hill we saw there were seven crosses. A naked man was fixed to each one of them. A detachment of Roman soldiers stood by to make sure sure there were no attempts at rescue. My father led me to the cross on which Simon was hanging.

Simon had been horribly scourged; the thongs of the whip had spared no part of his body. The blood had congealed in clots over the livid scars that now covered his milk-white skin. His legs, which were bound together, were contorted. His whole face had been so changed by his hours of anguish that I could hardly recognize him. For the time being it looked as if he had passed into a swoon. But I could tell from the rise and fall of his breast that he was still alive. I could not bear to look at him a second longer. I covered my eyes with my hands. But my father dragged my hands away and forced round my head so that I was facing Simon again.

'Look!' my father cried. 'There is your friend Simon. Observe the spectacle. Look at Simon carefully – because I never want you to forget what the Romans have done to him. For it is the Romans who have done all of this. A Roman Judge sentenced him to death by crucifixion. A Roman Procurator approved the sentence. Roman soldiers flogged him. Roman soldiers have nailed him and bound him to that cross to die in agony.'

While I now repeated my father's words to Caleb – the words my father had uttered over thirty years ago – I found I had covered my eyes, as if I were once again there on the hill, and as if darkness could obliterate what I had seen. But I would never be able to forget the horror of it. For, as my father spoke, Simon turned his head towards us. And as I saw his face, distorted by anguish, then I remembered. I remembered the dove with its broken leg down by the stream, and Simon's gentle hands. I do not know if Simon recognized me, because at that moment I fainted.

As I sat in my chair I became aware that I was still speaking to Caleb. I let my hands drop from my eyes. The vision was engraved on my mind, and there was nothing, now, that could remove it.

I was ill for a long time, I told Caleb. I could not sleep. The doctors thought I would die. But I survived. I survived – but in a curious way. I did not feel any more. I could experience neither love nor hate, nor joy nor sorrow. I ate and I drank. I was quite healthy in my body. And as I grew up I found ways of satisfying my body's needs. Later, when I was nineteen, more as a diversion than as a profession, I began to study medicine. Then my father died, and I found myself a rich man and my own master. I indulged my tastes in several ways. Rumours began to spread about my behaviour.

When my reputation in Jerusalem became too well known for safety I came to Galilee and bought this house by the lake. I could indulge myself within these walls in perfect security. My life here was one constant fulfilment of each need which arose in me. But as the months passed by, I began sometimes to feel a faint throb in my heart. Perhaps a small part of it had remained alive and was beginning to stir again. Then I realized that the punishment for complete selfishness is that the world becomes a desert. I had always tried to be kind, because I believed such behaviour was correct. I now wanted to love spontaneously. I wanted to find some person – somebody with whom I could feel at one. Someone like Raguel. So I tried.

The instant I mentioned Raguel my mind came back to the present. I was once again in the long room of my villa, overlooking the lake. I rose to refill Caleb's cup of wine and my own.

'I expect it was my fault,' I told Caleb. 'I tried too soon – before I was ready, before I was able to give enough. Whatever the reason, I failed. Over the years I found I was still unable to love. And then – then I began to see young Simon again, Simon with his russet hair and his arms spread out on the cross. And I remembered my father's words, "Never forget what the Romans have done to him". Then I thought of the Romans still ruling in the arrogance of their power throughout our land. Suddenly I felt a rage sweeping up into my empty heart, a rage against the Romans who defiled our country by their presence. So I thought: "If I cannot love, at least I can hate". I now began to spend more time in Jerusalem. Soon I was able to find men who shared my hatred and who were prepared to work carefully until the moment came to strike.'

I moved towards Caleb. 'Now do you understand why I wanted to see you?' I asked.

But even as I put the question I wondered if there was any point in trying to gain Caleb's support. For as I looked down at his graceful head and delicate neck and the soft features of his innocent face I became almost convinced that this slender young man might win the hearts of hundreds of simple-minded followers around the Lake of Galilee, but no amount of training or argument would ever make him lead a contingent against the Romans.

'Could you have wanted to see me because you thought I could help your hatred?' Caleb asked.

'Can you help me to love?' I demanded in reply.

'Perhaps,' Caleb answered quietly, looking at me steadily.

For one instant I forgot about my task and I forgot about Raguel. A vision had invaded my mind, and I could see myself stretched out beside Caleb. I was clasping him with one hand while I explored the softness of his body with the other. Abruptly I turned away from him and went to stand by the window. When I spoke I had already regained my dispassionate tone of authority.

'You must not suppose I am head of the group,' I told Caleb. 'I am an important member I admit, but I am not the chief. I take my orders like the rest of us. One of my orders was to meet you and sound you out.'

'The voice told me to prepare a way for the host of mankind,' Caleb answered. 'My orders were to announce the good news.'

'The same message was given to Isaiah,' I replied. 'And we are still not free.'

'But I should have told you,' Caleb said. 'The voice spoke to me yet a second time. You see, after I left the Essenes I wandered again for a while. I felt rather lost and unhappy. My mind was confused by all the teachings I had listened to. I knew that only solitude could heal me. Suddenly, one morning, to my wonderment and joy – I heard the voice once again. "All that was foretold will come true," the voice said. "The Messiah will be arrested and imprisoned. He will be scourged. He will be crucified. The Messiah must die by the very nature of his task." For a while there was silence in the desert where I stood. "But on the third day he will rise again," the voice continued. "He will arise from the dead. Then he will return to earth in glory to establish my reign forever".'

'I cannot believe the Messiah will come while Israel is enslaved,' I said quietly.

'I believe the Messiah is present in Israel, alive here today,' Caleb answered.

'How can he come to save us if we do nothing to deserve him?' I demanded.

Caleb glanced at me in surprise. 'Do you believe God's blessing comes only as a reward for good conduct?' he asked.

'How else?' I enquired.

'Do you believe that poverty and suffering are a divine punishment for sin?'

'We are told that it is not given to us to know,' I answered.

Caleb had been looking down at his glass of wine. He now raised his head. He spoke very gently.

'But I give it to you to know – as the poor of the world and the simple already know,' he said. 'God's special blessing will come to pitiable outcasts and sinners.'

'Caleb, you must listen to me,' I told him. 'We are all finally accountable to God. But we have an immediate duty. You may be right. God's Kingdom may come soon. But until that day, surely it is our duty to fight against oppression?'

'What is it you want me to do?' Caleb asked.

'When the moment arrives, persuade your followers to join in the conflict on our side,' I said. 'We might be able to give one or two of your men some training. But the moment has not come yet. Far from it. We must wait for at least a year or two until our movement gathers strength. The last thing we want is another unsuccessful riot against the Romans in Jerusalem. Any disturbance would only help Valerius Gratus, because it would give him, as Governor, the excuse to use the severest methods of repression throughout Palestine.'

'If it is God's intention that I should help you, the voice will tell me,' Caleb replied.

'So at present I cannot expect any assistance from you?' I enquired.

'Not in a revolt,' Caleb answered.

'What other help can I get from you?'

'Faith.'

'But I believe.'

'You believe in the God of revolt and retribution,' Caleb said. 'You do not believe in the God whose voice I hear – the God who asks for mercy, not for sacrifice.'

'My faith is in the God of Israel who will help us to kill our enemies,' I answered with a grim smile.

'Because you think you can only hate,' Caleb told me. 'Yet already you have shown you can trust. For, after all, you have trusted me. And that was faith of a kind. I said just now that I could perhaps help you to love. I am now sure I can.'

I was watching Caleb. I tried to read a meaning in the expression of his eyes. Suddenly I was so astonished that I nearly cried out aloud, because it seemed to me that in a flash I had seen a look of full complicity, as if Caleb knew the passion that had invaded me and sympathized and was prepared to assuage it. I tried to find a reason for the unexpected sign which I was almost certain I had received. In spite of his outward simplicity Caleb was ambitious in his own way. Could it be possible that for the sake of his cause and for the sake of his followers – many of whom must be near to starving – Caleb had decided to make a temporary compromise? Was that the meaning behind the look he had given me? For a while I was uncertain. I was silent. A few instants later as I examined Caleb's eyes, I realized that I had been mistaken, and I understood their constant message. His eyes expressed a forceful and completely innocent compassion.

'It would be no good,' I answered.

'I know the thought that has entered your mind,' Caleb said.

'Then you know why it would be useless,' I replied.

Caleb nodded. He took a sip of his wine.

'When we are first in love,' he said, half speaking to himself, 'we love what is God in the form of our beloved, what is God in the beauty of the person who is so dear to us. But when we have overcome desire, we are free to love what is God in that person's spirit. Even so, our beloved can only be a small reflection of God – just as a small mirror held in the hand can reflect the sun. Moreover, we can be betrayed by the mirror, for the tiniest flaw in it will cause distortion. Only by direct communication with God can we make certain that we may hope to see his complete and intricate glory.'

'But supposing we make the sacrifice of our earthly love,' I replied. 'Supposing, for example, we renounce the evident and splendid pleasures of the flesh, what if at the end of our lives we discover that the vision of God were a deception and a bitter sadness to us? What if the face of God as finally revealed to us in the moment of death were mean, ugly, revengeful, cruel and lacking in any compassion?'

'The God who made the mountains and the valleys and the flowers that grow on them, the God who created the birds of paradise and the lambs playing in green fields could not be ugly,' Caleb stated.

'The same God made scorpions, vultures and jackals. The same God made Man,' I told him. 'Oh, Caleb, be careful of your use of imagery! Do not let it lead you astray.'

Suddenly Caleb rose quietly from his chair and came up to me. He spoke in a low voice.

'Is there anyone in your household whom you do not trust?' he asked.

'Of course not,' I replied.

'Anyone who would betray you?'

I shook my head. 'Not possibly,' I said. 'Why do you ask?'

'Then it can be only from curiosity,' Caleb replied. 'The person has gone. But just now as you spoke, I am quite certain there was somebody listening at the door.'

'It's very unlikely,' I told him.

'Does no one here in Galilee know that you are involved in a plan of revolt?' Caleb asked.

'No one,' I replied. 'Not even Raguel.'

'I wish I could see more clearly,' Caleb said. 'I wish I could foretell your future, because I am afraid that what you are planning is very dangerous. When I held the ring from your finger I could see your past. I could see much of the present. But ahead there was obscurity. So I cannot tell you what will happen to you in the future – even within the next few days. But let me ask you this. If your revolt began far sooner than you expected, would the Pharisees and Sadducees help you?'

'Some of them,' I replied. 'Many of the Pharisees, certainly. But our proclamation will be designed to appeal to all sects.' I smiled at Caleb. 'We can learn from your mistakes,' I added.

Caleb laughed. 'What mistakes would you say I made?'

'You appeal to the masses,' I stated. 'You offend the elect. You do not even trouble to observe the simplest ceremonial usages.'

'What usages?' Caleb enquired.

'You took food just now in this room without washing your hands,' I told him.

'I washed my hands this morning,' Caleb replied, grinning at me like a schoolboy. 'Surely that is enough?'

'Since then you have been in the market-place,' I reminded him.

'But my disciples kept the crowds away from me,' Caleb explained. 'I suppose someone could have touched my hand, so a Pharisee would have washed again. But can you possibly believe in that nonsense?'

'I am worried by your carelessness,' I informed him. 'Even out here in Galilee you must take great care not to announce your views too openly. A charge of blasphemy can very easily be brought. I have influence in the High Court of the Sanhedrin. But if they produced enough witnesses to prove your words, it would be very difficult to get an acquittal. And you see, Caleb, I may not be able to love, but already I am growing quite fond of you.'

'I am glad,' Caleb said.

'So be careful,' I warned him. 'Watch your words.'

'There is no need to wory about me,' Caleb said in a tone of conviction which at once impressed and alarmed me. 'The voice tells me what I am to do. And the voice has told me to expect a sign. "In this period, no more instructions", the voice said. "Only a sign".'

'What sign?' I asked. 'You are not a superstitious Roman. You cannot believe in signs and portents.'

'Last time when the voice spoke, I was told to expect a sign,' Caleb said. 'That is all.'

'If you are a true prophet, God's message should be clear to you,' I replied.

'I can see only fragments of truth,' Caleb explained. 'The odd pieces are sometimes ill-assorted. I can only tell you that on the day when you and I see the whole building of God's truth we will perceive how each stone and pillar fits into place.' Caleb paused in thought. 'This morning, in some odd way,' he continued, 'I felt the day was even closer than I had supposed.'

Again Caleb paused. As I watched the withdrawn look creep once more into his face, I decided finally that Caleb could never become the leader for whom we were searching to help our insurrection in Galilee. He had fire in his spirit and great enthusiasm. But his attitude towards life was far too simple and remote for politics – even for local politics. He moved in a world of his own making – a spiritual world which had no contact with everyday affairs. To a certain extent I believed he might well be inspired; he might truly hear a voice that spoke to him – as many spiritually-minded men have heard voices before him. He was, in fact, an unusual and perhaps abnormal young man with intense charm and considerable gifts. With his beguiling and passionate sincerity he might well gain a following amongst the outcasts and dispossessed of Galilee. His ideas might even be remembered for a while. But as Caleb grew older the inspiration of youth would leave him, common sense and the ordinary needs of living would cover his spiritual ardour as leaves cover a lawn; he would realize he was no longer any different from the breed of other men, and he would be glad to return to the security and simple life of the vineyard on the terraces above Cana.

We were both silent, each absorbed in his own thoughts. I heard the handle of the door leading to the inner courtyard turn, and Raguel walked into the room. Immediately I noticed the excitement in his face. He was in the mood I most dreaded – nervous, overwrought and exhilarated. Caleb had told me of his intuition that someone had been listening at the door. For a moment I wondered if it could have been Raguel. Then I tried to banish my disloyal suspicion.

'Please excuse me for interrupting your conversation together,' Raguel said. 'But I felt I must come back because I have something quite important to tell you both.' Raguel turned towards Caleb. 'But first I have an apology to make,' Raguel announced to him. 'I have to confess that when you came to the house this morning I am afraid I did not believe in you. I thought you were just one more of the false prophets we have seen around here these last ten years. In fact, I was convinced you were an impostor. So I am afraid I was lacking in respect. Please will you forgive my rudeness?'

'Of course,' Caleb replied.

I have known Raguel for over ten years. My ears are attuned to every shade of meaning which lies behind his tone of voice. I had at once detected the note of insincerity in Raguel's little speech to Caleb.

'Raguel, what are you trying to do?' I asked quietly.

'To be honest for once,' Raguel answered. He took three paces towards me. 'Do you want to know what changed my mind about Caleb?' he asked. 'Or are you afraid to find out?'

'There is no need to give the reason,' Caleb said quickly.

'Tell me,' I said to Raguel with deliberate calm. 'What changed your mind? I am not afraid to find out. On the contrary. I am very interested.'

'Raguel *has* changed his mind,' Caleb stated. 'That is what is important. Not the reason.'

'I want to know, Raguel,' I persisted.

'Very well,' Raguel said. And once again he turned towards Caleb. 'I was worried when I heard you had been invited to this villa,' he told him. 'I feared you might be a trouble-maker. One of my duties as Joseph's secretary and friend has always been to keep him out of any trouble, so I wanted to get rid of you as soon as I could. But I now know the truth about you, and I realize you must have seen my mistrust. You must have been aware I was against you.'

'I could sense you disliked me,' Caleb replied. 'I could not understand the reason.'

'There were several reasons,' Raguel explained. 'I need only tell you the main one. I was afraid of your influence.'

' "Influence" might not be quite the correct word,' I observed, and I could hear the sarcasm in my voice. But Raguel ignored me.

'I was afraid that you might have some odd power which was evil,' he told Caleb. 'Then, when you were speaking to little Merab, I saw that your words were making an impression on her. You said she had gone into a cave to meet a young man called Ephron. You said she had given him something silver. Suddenly I remembered what Leah, our housekeeper, had told me earlier this morning. She was worried because a silver plate was missing from the store-chest.'

'I am afraid I cannot believe you,' I announced.

'Ask Leah when she comes back from the village,' Raguel replied.

'Indeed I will,' I answered. I could feel a faint anger rising in me.

'Then you told us there was something gold touching Merab's skin,' Raguel said to Caleb. 'So I decided it must mean the girl had stolen again. But because you had found out, she would be anxious to return the object – whatever it was. So when I left you and Joseph together, I went to my room but I kept watch. Presently I heard someone creeping along the passage. I flung open my door. I saw Merab. She had something in her hand. It was a gold spoon – one of a set of six that Joseph bought last time he was in Alexandria.'

'How could Merab have opened the store-chest?' I asked.

'She had a key – a key which had been made for her by the young man she met,' Raguel answered. 'You still do not believe me, do you?'

'No, Raguel,' I replied. 'I do not.'

'Merab,' he called out. 'Come here.'

I was beginning to understand what Raguel was trying to do, but I could not discern any reason for it. I glanced towards Caleb. For the first time he seemed unhappy and worried. Merab came in. She was pale with fear.

'Merab,' Raguel ordered. 'Show your master the gold spoon I found in your hand.'

Merab held out the spoon towards me. Her hand was quivering. I took the spoon and examined it. Raguel was right. It belonged to a set I had bought recently in Alexandria.

'Did you steal this?' I asked her.

The girl lowered her head. 'Yes, sir,' she mumbled.

'How did you open the store-chest?' I enquired.

'I had a key,' Merab answered. 'Ephron made a key for me.'

'Ephron made it. Surely you can remember young Ephron?' Raguel asked me in a kind of triumph. 'We took him on as a gardener for a time. But we sent him away because we suspected he was a thief. You must remember him? Very tall and dark-skinned. Rather handsome in a coarse way.'

'Yes,' I answered. 'I can remember.'

I looked towards Caleb. I wondered if he would be pleased that his power of divination had been proved exact, but he was staring down at the floor, and his face was sad. I turned back to Merab. 'So you have been stealing things from this house and bringing them to Ephron?' I asked.

Merab began to cry. 'He promised he would marry me,' she said. 'I loved him, and I believed in him.' She gave a low moan. 'But I got afraid,' she blurted out. 'I was afraid of him. Please forgive. I was going to put the spoon back. I swear I was. Please forgive me, sir.'

'Now do you believe what I said?' Raguel demanded.

'Please forgive me,' Merab continued moaning.

'I can forgive,' I told her. 'However, I must warn you that Leah will not forgive so easily. But Ephron is the one who must be caught and punished.'

Caleb had been standing motionless by the window. Suddenly he spoke. 'Ephron is dead. I know it,' he said abruptly. 'Less than an hour ago – yes, less than an hour – he was killed in the cave.'

Merab gave a cry. Caleb moved towards her.

'I am afraid he is dead, Merab,' he said. 'There were three or four of them . . . Robbers from the hills. He died quickly . . . Grieve now, Merab. Grieve now, for you will regret when you can grieve no longer.'

The girl's whole body was shaken by the violence of her sobbing.

'You may go now, Merab,' I told her. 'I will try to persuade Leah to be lenient with you.'

Merab nodded her head to show that she had heard me and stumbled out of the room. I turned to look at Caleb. He was trembling and tense. I had noticed that once Caleb had reached a state of mind when his powers of perception started to work he remained in that elated condition for some time. He had now begun to stare at Raguel.

'It was you,' he told him. 'You were listening at the door.'

Raguel hesitated. 'Yes,' he answered after a pause.

'That cannot be true,' I protested.

'I am afraid it is,' Raguel replied.

'But why?' I asked in amazement and disgust. 'Why did you listen?'

'To find out what had come between us,' Raguel answered. 'Could you not trust me? Did it need a prophet to inspire trust in you?'

'A prophet!' I exclaimed.

'Yes,' Raguel replied. 'I used the word "prophet". For he is indeed a prophet. I am now certain.'

'How can you possibly be certain?' I asked. But Raguel was no longer listening to me. He had turned to Caleb and was contemplating him with a look of reverence.

'You are a prophet,' he said to Caleb. 'I am sure of it now. So you must know my sadness and the reason for it. Help me, Caleb. Help me, Master.'

I was determined not to let Raguel see how much his use of the word 'Master' to Caleb had angered me.

'Raguel, you are a poet,' I told him. 'You have a keen imagination, as all your friends know. You must not allow your fancies to upset your reason.'

'But I *can* call him "Master" now, for I believe,' Raguel answered quietly. 'I believe in him. I consider that Caleb belongs in the company of the prophets. And even more. I believe it can well be possible that he may have been chosen. I believe he may be the host of all mankind about whom he spoke. He may be the Anointed One. How can either of us tell?'

Caleb's eyes were open wide in astonishment.

'The Anointed One,' Caleb repeated in a whisper.

'Do not believe him, Caleb,' I said.

'What reason have I to lie?' Raguel demanded.

'I am uncertain of the reason,' I replied. 'I cannot give you the reason. Yet I am certain you are lying.'

I looked towards Caleb. He did not appear to have heard what I had said to Raguel. He was standing rigid and perfectly still. He seemed to have forgotten our presence.

'Not yet. It is not yet,' he murmured to himself. 'When Raguel spoke then, I thought it might be the sign. But it is not yet. It is soon, though. Very soon. For I have been in this room before . . . Perhaps in some dream . . . I have heard Raguel's words before. I have known this moment before – this moment of intensity, this moment when all the currents of my life seem to have flowed towards this point of time – this instant, when I see Joseph staring at me, as if he thought I was mad, and Raguel, like me, waiting for a sign to convince him . . . I have known this moment before. This moment when the sun falls on the courtyard, and the cypress trees stand motionless like statues. And there, above the silence, I can hear the beating of my heart.'

Caleb was silent. He stood gazing out at the courtyard, lost in some mystic imagining.

'What have you done, Raguel?' I asked. 'You do not believe in Caleb. I know it, because I know you.'

'We all change, Joseph. You said so yourself just now,' Raguel answered. 'You changed because you could not love. I changed because I needed proof in order to believe in God. And at last I have found it.'

I could feel the anger burning my cheeks. 'You are arguing for Caleb's benefit,' I told Raguel. 'Not for mine.'

'But you have seen proof, Joseph,' Raguel replied. 'If Caleb were not inspired how could he have known about Merab's theft and her visit to Ephron?'

'He has prophetic gifts of divination,' I answered. 'Nothing more. And I would advise you to recognize the fact.'

'Why are you afraid to believe in him?' Raguel enquired. 'Can it be because you are afraid to believe that the Kingdom of God may come quite soon? Is it because in your own mind you prefer the Kingdom as it now exists in Jerusalem – the Kingdom of the Sanhedrin?'

'Be careful, Raguel,' I warned.

'Careful!' Raguel exclaimed, his voice rising in hysteria. 'What else have I been these last ten years? Careful to please, careful not to annoy, careful of your needs, your household, your securities, your wealth. I tell you, Joseph, I am the most careful man in Galilee.'

For a while Raguel and I looked at each other. I tried to control my rage. I made myself remember my friendship with Raguel over the long years. I remembered the enchanting young boy whom I had taken back to my house. I recalled his eagerness and charm. I reminded myself of his companionship and loyalty. I forced myself to acknowledge that though Raguel was no longer my lover, I was still very fond of him. Certainly I did not wish him ever to leave me.

'Very well, Raguel,' I said. 'I expect I was wrong to threaten.'

The apology calmed him as I intended it would.

'I expect I did wrong to deserve a threat,' he muttered.

Once again I looked towards Caleb. He was still standing by the far window. He was examining the small table in the corner with a curious intensity.

'This servant Manasseh made this table,' he said to himself. 'He brought them the table this morning.'

Caleb fingered the wood of the inlay. He still spoke aloud, though

69

I felt certain he was unconscious of the two of us within the room.

'This morning . . . That is part of it,' he continued. 'The moment is very near now . . . The dream is coming back to me . . . The voice spoke to me in a dream. That is it. But because it was a dream, I remembered it only vaguely afterwards. And I was not certain. But I am sure now. I am very sure . . . I was in this room, and so was Joseph, and so was Raguel. And little Merab had been standing there crying. And the voice said. The voice . . . Oh God, oh God, I remember now! Yes, I can remember.'

Caleb raised his head. His face was alight with ecstasy.

'Now, God. Yes, now,' he cried out. 'Now is the moment . . . You said, oh God, you said, "I will give the sign, Caleb. You will visit this room. You will stand by the small table, and in it – inside the drawer – you will find the sign I have sent for you, Caleb. You will find the sign that will make you sure of your calling. This sign will confirm to you that you have been chosen to be the host – the host of all mankind. And this is what the sign will be. The sign will be a plain cross. It will be in the table's drawer. A plain cross of wood. You will find it inside the drawer. And when you find it, then you will know. All your doubts will vanish, and you will know for certain. You will know that you are the Chosen One." '

Caleb stopped speaking. Very slowly he stretched out his right hand and pulled open the drawer of the table. From it he took out a small wooden cross in the shape of a T. At that time, I did not know how the object had come to be there, but already I suspected that Manasseh must have made it. Caleb stared at the cross with wonder and awe. Then he lowered his head in submission, as a slave might do to his master.

'You will know you are the Messiah,' he concluded in a whisper.

There was silence in the room. When Caleb lifted his head, his eyes were misty with tears.

'Oh God, let me not fail,' he called out in supplication. 'Let me fulfil my task. Let me not falter. But never leave me, oh God. Never forsake me.'

I moved towards Caleb. I spoke very softly, for he was still in a trance.

'Caleb,' I said. 'Caleb, it was only a dream.'

Vaguely I was aware of the sound of the front door opening.

'Oh God, let me be worthy,' Caleb whispered.

'It was a dream, Caleb,' I repeated. 'Listen to me, Caleb. You must listen.'

The door from the outer courtyard opened, and Leah came in. Evidently she had just returned from the market, for she was carrying her shopping bag. Ben and Gomer followed her into the room. As Leah came closer, I observed there was a strange expression of excitement on her face I had not seen before. Quietly Leah moved straight towards Caleb and stood in front of him. Her plump face was shining, and for all her stoutness there was something about her attitude which reminded me of a child. Caleb was still dazed, but when he became aware of Leah's presence he looked at her enquiringly. It was obvious he had never seen her before. Leah raised her hands and joined the palms of them together in salutation. For an instant, neither Raguel nor I could understand what was so unusual about her greeting to Caleb. Then we gasped in amazement. Leah's right arm was raised beside her left. Slowly she knelt down at Caleb's feet.

'This is Leah, their housekeeper,' Ben told Caleb, stammering with excitement. 'She touched your hand, Master. Leah pressed forward through the crowd and touched your hand when you were in the market-place this morning. And at that very moment her arm was healed.'

'Her arm has been useless for over twenty years,' Gomer babbled. 'Touching you cured her. She has been round to see all her friends in the village to show them, Master. Every one of them, haven't you, Leah?'

'Her arm used to hang stiff at her side. And now look, Master! Look!' Ben cried. He turned to Raguel and then to me. 'This is a miracle, I tell you,' he proclaimed.

Leah gazed up at Caleb. 'You have healed me, my Lord and my Master,' she told him quietly. 'From this day I will bear proof of it.'

When Caleb spoke, his face seemed transfigured with joy.

'I have healed you, Leah,' he said. 'I have come to heal all those who believe in me. I have come to lead the world from darkness into light. I have come to redeem all sins and wash away all evil, to bring peace to those who grieve and happiness to those who are oppressed. I have come as the Son of the Living God to redeem his people. For I am indeed the long-expected one. I have come to prepare the way of God, my father in heaven. I am the long-awaited Teacher of Righteousness. I am the Messiah.'

There was silence. Ben and Gomer were staring at Caleb in awe. Raguel had lowered his head as if in prayer. Suddenly Gomer gave a little gasp as the full import of what Caleb had said struck him, and he flopped down on to his knees. Ben nodded his head, then knelt down beside Gomer.

'I am the Messiah,' Caleb repeated softly.

'No, Caleb,' I said.

'I am the Redeemer foretold by the prophets,' Caleb continued. 'And all prophecy will be fulfilled.'

'You have healed Leah because she believed in your powers of healing,' I told him. 'You are a healer with prophetic gifts. But nothing more.'

'I am the Son of God,' Caleb answered.

I looked around at the four of them in the room in their attitudes of reverence. There was not one of them who could help me shake this deluded young man from his present mystic conviction. I knew I must wake him from his trance before it was too late.

'Then do you suppose you are our legitimate King?' I asked loudly. 'Are you the Son of David? Do you lay claim to the throne of Israel?'

'Yes,' Caleb answered.

'What idiotic nonsense!' I cried out. 'What stupid arrogance! And if you are so unhinged in mind as to proclaim yourself the Messiah, what good will it do you or anyone else? What help do you suppose you will get in your mission, and from whom will you receive it? If you go to any centre of Judaism and proclaim yourself the Messiah, the crowds will tear you into pieces.'

'If any man tried to harm me before I had accomplished my mission,' Caleb replied, 'the very hills would cry out in protest.'

'You must be mad!' I exclaimed. 'No one – apart from a few of your disciples – will believe in you for an instant. The mass of the people and the powers of the land will revile you in disgust and horror.'

'All prophecy will be fulfilled,' Caleb said. 'I will go to Jerusalem to preach the words of God my father.'

'If all prophecy is to be fulfilled,' I told him sarcastically, 'it is unfortunate that you have an elder brother and that you were born in Cana – not in Bethlehem. Moreover, if prophecy is to be fulfilled, you will have to leave your visit to Jerusalem until next year. For the

72

days of the Passover, as you well know, finished two months ago.'

But Caleb did not listen to me. He was staring at the cross which was clutched in his right hand.

'I shall preach in the temple,' he announced in a voice of exaltation. 'I shall be arrested. I shall be tried and found guilty. I shall be whipped. I shall be crucified.'

'Yes, Caleb,' I said. 'One thing is certain. If you go to Jerusalem surely you will be crucified.'

'I shall be crucified. I shall die, and I shall be buried,' Caleb proclaimed.

Then he paused, and as he now spoke his eyes gleamed with the wonderful triumph of prophetic inspiration which it was evident at that instant possessed his whole being.

'But on the third day I shall rise from the dead,' Caleb continued. 'Just as a blade of corn is cut down but springs up again to the song of birds, so I shall be cut down and buried, but I shall arise from death. And when I return to earth the birds will sing, and the stars will blaze like a thousand suns.'

By now Caleb had reached a state of frenzy. I felt that for his own sake I must force him back to reality.

'You *will* be crucified,' I told him. 'But first they will strip you naked and scourge you with a whip of leather thongs. Do you hear, Caleb? The whip has small pieces of metal and bone tied to each thong, and they will tear your flesh.'

I was not certain if Caleb had heard me. He was breathing heavily, and his eyes were curiously glazed.

'They who are put to death for the sake of God will arise to life,' Caleb said. 'So I will arise from the dead, and I will join my father in heaven.'

Caleb would have continued speaking, but I interrupted him, raising my voice so that it was louder than his words.

'You will be scourged, Caleb,' I repeated. 'And after the public has gloated over your pain and degradation, an inscription recording your offence of blasphemy will be put around your neck. You will then be led to the wooden cross on which you are to be fastened. Still naked, you will be forced to pick up the cross, and they will make you carry it along the winding road that leads up to the hill.'

I paused. I hoped that what I had said might have pierced through to Caleb's consciousness. But he was still imprisoned by his trance.

'Then will come the day of judgment, and I will return to earth with my father,' he cried in a tone of ecstasy. 'We will return in power and glory with all the angels of heaven. And those who have died in grief will arise in joy. And those who were poor will be made rich. And those who have been killed for the sake of God will awake to life.'

I went up to Caleb. I took his head between my hands and turned it towards me so that his misted, blue eyes were staring at me.

'Listen to me,' I said. 'When you have reached the hill, you will put down the cross,' I continued. 'Then you will be made to lie down beside it. Next, you will be tied to it. First, your hands will be nailed down. Then your feet will be bound to the cross. Already, a large, thick wooden peg will have been fixed into the upright beam of the cross. On this peg the weight of your body will rest when the cross is hauled up by ropes into position. The peg will stick out between your legs like an obscene phallus.'

As I now spoke I pressed my hands hard against Caleb's face. For an instant his eyes became aware of my presence. Then he seemed to be carried away once again into his rapture.

'At last will come peace on earth,' he cried. 'There will be no more hunger and no more hatred. There will be no more murder and no more war. Oh God, send me the words I should use when I preach. Send me the words, oh God, so I can give your message clearly.'

With my right hand I now began to tap gently against the side of his cheek. Once more his eyes seemed to become vaguely aware of me.

'Caleb,' I said, 'listen to me. At least try to understand the anguish which will most surely lie ahead of you if you go to Jerusalem and announce that you are the Messiah. They are certain to arrest you. They are certain to condemn you to crucifixion – and remember that I have been to the hill and seen a crucifixion. Death, I tell you, seldom occurs before thirty-six hours. On occasions a man has lived on the cross for nine days. Death is usually a long business, so a centurion and three of four soldiers are left on guard to prevent a rescue. The position of a man on the cross strains his whole body as if he were on a rack. The haemorrhage, caused by the nails piercing the hands, soon stops. The arteries of the head and stomach – so I can assure you as one who knows something of medicine – become overcharged with blood. Unimagined pains start in the head and in the heart. Slowly and eventually fever begins to set in, and gradually the limbs become rigid.'

Caleb gazed at me blankly. Between my hands I could feel the sweat running down his cheeks.

'Bless those who are penitent,' he said, speaking haltingly. 'Yes. Bless those who are poor. Yes. Bless those who are gentle and humble. Bless all those who truly love their fellow men.'

The mystic fervour which had overcome Caleb was so strong that I wonder if he were even conscious of what he was saying.

'Bless the lepers and outcasts of the world,' he continued. 'Bless all those who repent.'

I struck his face with my hand. He remained motionless, but I could see that the mist had begun to leave his eyes.

'Who will bless them?' I demanded, suddenly and loudly, letting my hands drop to my sides.

For a moment Caleb's expression was confused as he gazed at me. But I knew he had heard my question, for his eyes, blue as the lake outside, were now unclouded.

'I, myself, can bless them,' Caleb answered.

'No,' I replied. 'You cannot. Only God can bestow blessing.'

'I can bless them,' Caleb said. 'I can give my blessing to whom I choose. For I am the Son of God.'

'What you are saying is blasphemy,' I warned Caleb.

I could feel anger beginning to swirl around my head, rising as as uncontrollably as a tide. For all his innocence Caleb's presumption in supposing he was the Messiah, the deliverer for whom our nation had waited so long, had started to enrage me.

'It is blasphemy,' I repeated.

'I can bless in God's name,' Caleb proclaimed. 'Because I am one with my father. I am part of God.'

This assumption of Godhead was so outrageous that for an instant I could not believe he could have uttered such a phrase.

'I am part of God,' Caleb said once again.

In my brain the tide of rage had swept over the last bulwark. I could feel myself trembling. I glanced down at my hands. They were shaking as if with palsy. With an effort I moved towards the staircase leading to the upper storey.

'I will hear no more blasphemy,' I said.

I began to climb the stairs. I could feel my heart thudding. I stopped and turned to Raguel.

'You will call Manasseh,' I told Raguel. 'He will escort all three guests from the house.'

In silence I climbed the stairs that led on to the landing. I walked along the passage to my room.

When I reached my room I lay down on a couch which I had placed so that I had a view of the lake. A gentle wind was shuffling across the water. White flecks glittered in the sunshine. As I reclined there, my heart was pounding, but the rage had started to empty from my head. I began to play with my signet ring, sliding it up and down my little finger. Gradually I became calmer, though I was still disturbed.

My immediate anxiety was concerned with Caleb. I knew the extent of my influence in the Sanhedrin; I was also aware of its general attitude towards our religion. This senate formed from a subject race to which I belonged was bigoted in the extreme. Without any doubt, if Caleb went to Jerusalem and proclaimed himself the Messiah he would be arrested and killed. One could, of course, hope that when the trance left him Caleb would appreciate the danger ahead. But I had been alarmed by the intensity of Caleb's fervour. He was sincere – most certainly; he possessed most unusual powers of divination; he was a mystic; he might even be a true healer – unless Leah's seemingly miraculous cure had been caused – as I now suspected – by some violent hysterical reaction. The trouble was that the popularity of his teaching in the district, combined with an unfortunate series of events, had deluded Caleb into a fantastic and blasphemous belief. He was an extremely attractive and beautiful young man whose gifts might well destroy him, unless some method could be found of making him appreciate the truth.

So long as his delusions lasted, Caleb was a menace both to himself – and to me. For if Caleb went to Jerusalem there would almost surely be a riot before the senate police arrested him. And a riot would give Valerius Gratus an opportunity to impose far stricter controls over us.

I knew Valerius Gratus. He was an affable man, both witty and urbane in a cynical way. He was also ambitious. He intended to rise far beyond the position of Procurator over a land which in his eyes was no more than a sub-province of Syria. He had therefore determined to prove to the powers in Rome that he was capable and efficient. He was present in Palestine to keep the people subdued; he would use every means to do so. A riot would excuse far more severe methods of repression. A widespread riot could delay our plan indefinitely. This would be a disaster, for we had worked on the scheme for several years, and its execution depended on the positions likely to be held on the day of action by various of our leaders.

Thinking of our plan made me remember Raguel's odd behaviour. First, he had listened from behind the door to my conversation with Caleb. This in itself was odd. For, though he was not religious Raguel had formed his own code of behaviour over the years, and he adhered to it strictly. I knew that he considered the act of eavesdropping mean and indecent. Therefore the fact that he had broken his code showed plainly the extent to which his mind was now perturbed. His words to me earlier this morning should have warned me. But because I did not want to admit to myself that my relationship with Raguel was strained, I had disregarded his hysterical outburst. Something had been worrying Raguel *before* Caleb had appeared.

Surely, I reasoned to myself, surely after all those years Raguel must have confidence in me? Surely he cannot suppose that because I no longer make love to him I no longer care for him? He must know I am deeply fond of him. Why then should he be so upset? Because he is growing older? Because the brilliance of his looks is slightly fading? What else can he have expected as the years passed by? Because he is discontented with his poetry? Perhaps. Perhaps he is sad for both reasons. And this might explain his outburst. Quite possibly. But what could conceivably explain his sudden change of attitude towards Caleb? What could have been his motive?

I have known Raguel for over ten years. I can perceive each shade of meaning that lies behind his particular tone of voice. I know – at least I think I know – almost every twist and every alley in his devious mind. Most certainly I know when Raguel is sincere and when he is acting. I trust my eyes and my ears to judge the degree of his sincerity. So far, my judgment has always proved correct. I cannot believe it should have failed to be accurate this morning. When Raguel came back into the room and addressed Caleb in tones of reverence and awe, I am certain his performance was false. His voice lacked candour; his gestures lacked sincerity. He was acting well, but I could see into his contrived little speeches and carefully arranged movements.

Raguel must have been aware of the risk that I myself would most probably detect the insincerity of his words, therefore his intention must have been to deceive Caleb. But why? Why should Raguel want Caleb to think that he believed in his divinity? For what purpose?

I had reached a possible solution to the puzzle when there was a knock at the door of my bedroom. I knew the rhythm of that knock.

'Come in, Raguel,' I said.

As soon as Raguel came into the room, I saw that he was still over-excited and distraught. From long experience I knew I should speak quickly before he began some hysterical tirade.

'Please sit down,' I said quietly, pointing to a chair close to my couch. 'I must talk to you about a matter of importance.'

In silence Raguel sat down and stared at me with his faded blue eyes.

'First, I must ask you a question,' I began. 'My question is simple. It is this. Have you listened at the door of a room in which I was having a conversation *before* today?'

'No,' Raguel answered. 'Never.'

'Then why did you listen at the door this morning?'

'I told you,' he replied. 'I wanted to find out what had come be-tween us.'

'And did you find out?'

'Most certainly.'

'What, then, was it that you discovered?'

'First, I found that you no longer trusted me,' Raguel answered. 'For some reason you have lost confidence in my loyalty. I am sup-posed to be your closest friend. Yet is seems that for the last two years you have kept the most important part of your activities a secret from me. I am trustworthy enough to handle your money affairs. Oh yes. I know that is so. I can be trusted with money. But when it comes to a matter that might cost you your life, then the shutter comes down. You don't consider me reliable. So the side of your life that counts most is kept secret from me, for I am no longer dependable. Yet within an hour – within only an hour – of conversing with a young preacher whom you have never even met before, you reveal to him facts which if repeated to the authorities would lead to your arrest and condemnation – senator or not. You have amazed me, Joseph . . . And when I heard your voice disclosing your innermost secret, how do you expect that I felt? If you had deliberately tried to wound and offend me – to prove that you considered me cheap and worthless – you could not have been more successful than you were this morning.'

Raguel sat back in his chair. I noticed his hands were quivering. I had expected an outburst of this kind, and I had determined my reply to it.

'Raguel,' I began, 'did you hear me give a brief outline of my plan to Caleb?'

'Yes.'

'So you heard me explain to Caleb that I had been *ordered* to meet him and sound him out?'

'I heard you tell him something to that effect,' he answered.

'But you do not believe it?' I enquired.

'Joseph, you may consider me untrustworthy, but please do not suppose that I am a fool,' Raguel said. 'Caleb may have been taken in by your talk of his becoming a leader of this district. I am not.'

'Why do you not believe it?'

'Why? Why indeed!' Raguel cried. 'I can tell you very simply, Joseph. If you really wanted a popular leader for the district, have there not been *other* preachers who have come to the lake and swayed the multitudes? You know there have been dozens of them. And have you ever invited a single one of those preachers to the house? No. Not one. But then most of those self-styled prophets have been old or ugly, emaciated and pock-marked or deformed. Their bloodshot eyes and matted hair and filthy robes would have disgusted you. But then Caleb appears on the shores of the lake and begins to preach. And someone – who was it, I wonder – someone tells you of the extreme beauty of the young man. And suddenly you see your chance. You invite him to the house. You are immediately attracted to him. Suddenly you see a way by which you can join the young man to that part of your existence you have kept secret from me. You discover a clever means of binding him to you. So you try to persuade him to join in your plan of revolt which will take many years to mature – years during which you can meet the young man constantly.'

I shook my head. 'You are very much mistaken, Raguel,' I told him.

'I wish I *were* mistaken,' he answered. 'But I saw and heard the proof of it all. That was the second thing I discovered this morning. You are unfaithful, Joseph. You are disloyal. When you no longer wanted me as a lover, you told me your nature had changed, and I tried to believe you – even though I remarked that your journeys to Alexandria still continued. However, at least your eyes never yearned after a young man in my presence. But this morning – this morning, Joseph – I saw you looking at Caleb, and I knew the meaning of that look. And later I heard your words to him.'

I rose from the couch and went to the window and stood gazing out at the lake. I wanted time to gather my thoughts. Presently I turned back to Raguel.

'You are uncertain if you believe in God,' I said to him. 'But you know very well that I do believe. So will you accept as the truth words that I promise before God are true?'

'Yes,' Raguel answered.

'Then I promise you before God that I was indeed instructed to sound out Caleb,' I said. 'His good looks had nothing to do with it.'

For a while Raguel was silent.

'But you were still attracted to him,' he said.

'Yes', I replied. 'I could not help being attracted to him.' Then I stopped and looked straight at Raguel.

'Nor could you,' I added.

As I spoke, I could see the flush spreading upwards from his slender neck.

'And does it matter so very much?' I continued quickly. 'We are both aware of our inclinations. Why should one of us take offence if the other is attracted by an unusually handsome young man? Did we quarrel when Ben first appeared at the villa? You know we did not. So why should we quarrel now – particularly when there are far more important matters to settle?'

I walked across to Raguel and put my hand on his shoulder.

'For the sake of our long friendship,' I told him, 'for the sake of our deep relationship, you must listen to me. Will you listen?'

Raguel stared into my eyes. Then he sighed, and I knew that his outburst of bitterness was over.

'Yes,' he answered.

'Then first you must understand that I wanted to tell you of my plan,' I explained. 'But the rules of our organization prevented it – because our leaders indeed know that discovery would lead to their death. For that reason I must now ask you to promise me solemnly that you will keep all you have heard secret. Will you promise me, Raguel?'

'Yes,' he answered. 'You know I will.'

'Next,' I said, 'I need your help with the problem of Caleb. And you are in a good position to aid me, for I am almost sure that Caleb is now convinced you wish to be one of his followers.'

'Joseph, I must explain,' Raguel began. But I interrupted him.

'There is no need to explain,' I said gently. 'Already I have worked out your reasoning. You pretended to believe in Caleb so that he would be persuaded he was indeed a prophet – if not the Messiah – and would accordingly go to Jerusalem. Once he reached Jerusalem, you were almost certain he would be arrested and thus be put out of our way.'

'I was afraid, Joseph,' Raguel muttered. 'I was afraid for both of us. And in consequence I think I may have done a terrible thing. If Caleb now goes to Jerusalem and is crucified I will be guilty for his death.'

'No,' I said firmly. 'Even if I fail to dissuade Caleb and he does go to Jerusalem, you will not be guilty. For how could you have foreseen the sequence of events? How could you have known that his power of divination would lead him to discover the wooden cross inside the drawer of the table? How could you tell that his power of healing would restore the nerve in kind Leah's arm? No, Raguel. You could not have foreseen the result of your action. But we shall both feel guilty if we do not now use all the means we can find to prevent Caleb going to Jerusalem.'

'How can we stop it?' Raguel asked. 'Already by now the news of the miraculous healing of Leah's arm will be known throughout the district. Soon it will spread to every village around the lake.'

'Certainly.'

'And by now Caleb has most likely proclaimed himself the Messiah – here in the market-place – and even if there is not an immediate riot, the news will spread like a fire.'

'No,' I said. 'For there will have been no proclamation.'

'But you heard him only a short while ago.'

'I heard him,' I replied. 'I was also watching the expression on the faces of Ben and Gomer.'

'What expression?'

'When Caleb announced he was the Messiah they were at first alarmed – not so much for themselves as for him. For they know the danger of such a proclamation. But they knelt down to him because of the force of his words and the intensity of his emotion. And I suppose they believed him. But then, when Caleb told us that he was a *part* of our very God, both Ben and Gomer – even though they are his

81

disciples – were shocked. I saw it. So I think they may try to persuade him to delay his announcement – though I admit it is unlikely he will heed them. Secondly, I believe Caleb himself will decide that he should wait until he reaches Jerusalem before he reveals himself. Thirdly, I think that some of my words of warning may have struck through to Caleb's consciousness. So, although it may only be short, we most likely have a period of time in which to act.'

'But what can we do?' Raguel asked. And I was glad that he had said 'we', for it made me sure that the danger to our friendship was beginning to diminish.

'First, we must discover what Caleb intends to do,' I replied. 'This afternoon I want you to go to see him and find out his plans.'

Raguel shifted uneasily, and I held his shoulder more firmly.

'Am I to keep up the pretence?' he asked.

'No,' I answered. 'There is no need for it.'

'Then, if he questions me, what am I to tell him?'

'Tell him you have had time for reflection,' I said. 'Tell him you have been considering the utterances of our prophets in the past with regard to the coming of the Messiah. Tell him that, as a result, you would like to believe in him, but cannot. What you say may help to bring Caleb to his senses.'

I moved my hand from Raguel's shoulder and brushed it lightly across his face. I smiled at him.

'And now,' I said, 'I am sure you must be feeling as hungry as I am. So let us go and eat.'

CHAPTER THREE

Why cannot I reconcile my judgment with my behaviour? I know that I am devoted to Joseph, so why should a part of me rebel against him, seek to annoy him, attempt to be free from his influence – when I am content to be his secretary and companion? And why in my moments of excitement or anger should I commit actions which my judgment tells me are wrong or foolish – even at the moment I am committing them? Why cannot I be single-minded and steadfast?

Perhaps the answer lies in the confusion of my nature, which is torn between the instincts of a man and desires which must more properly belong to a woman.

As I walked down to the village that afternoon I felt less disturbed and unhappy, for Joseph had done all that he could to reassure me. He had ordered a bottle of wine from his own vineyard to be opened, and we had finished it together. And during our meal he had talked on subjects which he knew always interested me – poetry and music, the art of tapestry, Greek philosophy. Joseph had been so pleasant and beguiling that I had almost forgotten the task ahead of me.

The village streets were empty. I went into a weaver's shop and discovered from the owner that Caleb was preaching on the shore. I took the narrow cobbled street that ran between little flat-roofed houses to the fishing-harbour. The wind had dropped, and the surface of the lake was very smooth. A few hundred yards along the beach I could see crowds of people clustered on the shore. A man was standing in the prow of a boat close to the shore, preaching to them. It was Caleb. I could recognize the white robe with the patches of bright-coloured stuffs sewn on to it. As I drew near I could hear some of his words, and I knew that Joseph's opinion had been correct. As yet Caleb had not proclaimed himself the Messiah. I also perceived that the news of the healing of Leah's arm had spread, for among the crowds were several cripples and hunchbacks, and women holding up deformed or sickly children. In the boat with Caleb was Ben, holding the oars, and behind him was sitting a sullen-looking young fisherman called Nathanael who was tall and brawny. I wondered if he were another disciple. I approached unobtrusively and listened.

'I tell you all yet again,' Caleb was saying, 'I am not a healer of bodies. Believe me. I cannot heal your bodily infirmities. That is not my purpose. I have been sent to heal your minds, to bring you comfort of spirit and peace, to announce to you the good tidings that the Kingdom of God is near at hand. And I can promise you that when that day comes, as it will very soon, there will be no more infirmities or suffering, no more hunger or thirst. And all mankind will rejoice, all living creatures will praise God, all earthly things will glorify God. The waters will sing his praise. The vineyards will shine with thick bunches of grapes. And in the fields, the wheat will grow as high as the cedars of Lebanon. And the hearts of all mankind will be filled with the love of God.'

Caleb paused. As he looked around at his audience, the slanting rays of the sun gleamed on the softness of his face. His expression was serene and tranquil. At that moment his beauty was at once profound and alarming in its dazzling brilliance.

'The Kingdom of God is near,' Caleb repeated. 'Therefore nothing else can matter – neither riches, nor jewels, nor mansions, nor any possessions. It is the spirit that lies in your heart which will survive. So do not fret yourself about money. Do not worry about what you will eat or drink or about what clothes you will wear. Do not worry, I tell you. Set your minds on God's Kingdom. Trust in God. Do not be concerned with anything else.'

As Caleb spoke I saw that Gomer had noticed my presence and was edging his way towards me through the crowd. I did not wish to meet him at that moment, so I turned away and walked quickly along the shore. As soon as I thought I was out of sight I slackened my pace. Presently I sat down on a boulder and watched the sun setting behind grey banks of clouds which were fringed with a golden light. I began to consider what I had seen and heard. Caleb had changed in the past six hours, I decided. He now spoke with less intensity, but with so much greater authority and certainty that I was sure he was now convinced – once and for all – that he was the Messiah. He was calm, yet elated and confident in his joyfulness.

I was wondering how Joseph could possibly hope to prevent Caleb from going to Jerusalem, when I heard a sound behind me. I turned and saw Gomer. He smiled at me apologetically.

'Good evening, sir,' he said. 'I saw you moving away from the crowd, and I thought you might not object if I joined you for a little talk, so I followed. I hope I'm not disturbing you?'

Gomer's jowls quivered anxiously as he smiled at me once again. There was something so blatantly dishonest about Gomer's obsequiousness that eventually one became convinced it was a double-bluff and ended up by believing him to be sincere.

'You are not disturbing me,' I said. 'Come and sit down.'

'Thank you, sir,' Gomer said, and he lowered himself cautiously on to a small mound of grass close to me. When he had settled down he peered at me with his bleary eyes.

'I am very much afraid that His Excellency, the senator, was upset by what took place this morning,' Gomer announced.

'He was indeed,' I answered.

'You did not kneel,' Gomer began cautiously. 'You did not join us, when Ben and I knelt down. But you lowered your head as if – as if you also believed in Caleb.'

'I believe he is a sincere and inspired man,' I replied.

'But you do not think he may possibly be the Chosen One?' Gomer enquired. 'You don't believe he can perhaps be the Messiah the prophets have foretold?'

'I thought he might be,' I said slowly. 'But since then I have considered the prophecies of our scriptures, and I have decided I was wrong.'

'I see,' Gomer muttered. 'I can understand, of course. But I can't help being sorry. We need good friends at this moment – more than ever before.'

'Do *you* believe he is the Messiah?' I asked suddenly.

Gomer blinked rapidly several times. Then he gazed at me with sad eyes, as if in reproach for the bluntness of my question.

'Yes, indeed,' he answered. 'Indeed I do believe it. All eight of us believe it. Just consider what Caleb has done. Just think of it. He's performed miracles. He's cured men of lunacy. He's healed Leah's arm. His prophecies always turn out to be correct. And he has heard the voice of God. And God *does* speak through him, I know it. God told him to wait for a sign. And God sent the wooden cross into the table drawer. Caleb told us so. The cross was the sign to show that God has chosen him. Caleb has been chosen to be the host for all mankind.'

I was watching Gomer's face. His forehead was greasy with sweat, and his heavy cheeks were shivering with emotion. He looked absurd and hideous. His sincerity was embarrassing.

'The cross was put into the drawer by Manasseh,' I told him gently.

'Ah,' Gomer replied with a leer of triumph. 'Ah, but what prompted Manasseh to do so? Or rather *who* prompted him? Can you answer me *that*? You can't, you see. That's just it. You can't. Never mind, sir. You've a warm heart. You'll believe in Caleb in time, I'm sure you will.'

'In time for what?' I asked. 'In time to see him hanging on a cross?'

'But he won't stay long on the cross,' Gomer said. 'Because God will rescue him.'

'Is that what he tells you?'

'He says he will die quickly and be buried,' Gomer replied. 'But

God will raise him from the dead. And at that moment the Kingdom of God will come. And there will be paradise here on earth. And I shall sit on one side of his throne, and Ben will sit on the other.'

Gomer's obvious eagerness and childlike faith were very surprising. Perhaps, as with other superficially crafty men I had known, Gomer's slyness concealed a profound simplicity.

'Does Caleb still intend to go to Jerusalem?' I asked.

'Yes,' Gomer answered. 'He will leave the day after tomorrow. He wanted to leave the village even sooner. But Ben, Nathanael and I – and the rest of the disciples – have arrangements we must make before we can get away. We shall travel by night because he doesn't want crowds of people flocking after him. Only the eight of us are to go with him. He doesn't want to cause a disturbance in the city when he arrives. The voice will tell him when the moment comes for him to make his declaration. But there will only be the eight of his disciples there in Jerusalem.'

Gomer was silent, but his worn, bleary eyes were still turned towards me.

'And that is the point,' he said. 'That is why I followed you here, sir, and, I'm afraid, interrupted your thoughts. You see, there will only be eight of us with him, so each one of us will be a marked man. I mean, we shall be surrounding him when he preaches, so it will be known that we are his disciples.'

Once again Gomer paused. The sweat was now trickling down his nose.

'Every one of his prophecies has been correct so far,' Gomer continued. 'Every single one of them. And I'm sure they will continue to be accurate. But with regards to this last prophecy – and please understand that I'm speaking without any disloyalty – just for one instant, just suppose that the *entire* prophecy was not *wholly* accurate. Suppose there should be some element of time that has been forgotten? Suppose when he stands in the court of the temple and tells the crowds he is the Messiah, suppose they turn on him and try to kill him? I know the chance is unlikely. I keep telling myself that I must trust in each detail of his prophecy – because I know he is the Messiah. I'm certain of it. But what if they attack him in one of the courts of the temple? The eight of us would try to defend him. Of course we would. But that's what worries me. You see, I'm not good with my fists. Nor are Saddoc, Eleazar and Mathias, come to that.

86

We're more town-folk – or perhaps village-folk should I say. We're not tough fishermen like Ben, Nathanael and Manahem – or like Dan, the carpenter, come to that. And I never could abide the sight of blood, I confess it.'

Gomer mopped his face with the edge of his robe, and gazed at me.

'So this, sir, is where I thought you could help us,' he said. 'I'm aware that His Excellency was angry this morning. But he's a good and generous man. And he has much influence in Jerusalem. I've heard this from many sources. Do you think you could possibly approach His Excellency on our behalf? On behalf of us disciples, I mean? Could you arrange for us to have some form of protection? I've been to Jerusalem. Indeed, I have. I've been there for the Feast of the Passover on several occasions. I know that the Sanhedrin, the senate perhaps I should say, has its own police. So this is what I wondered. Do you think that in his great generosity of heart His Excellency might possibly arrange for a unit of the senate police to be on the ready to stop any riot when we reach Jerusalem?'

Gomer paused again and looked at me with a beseeching glance of entreaty.

'Even a few of the police,' he said, 'even a few men might save our lives.'

I rose to my feet. Immediately Gomer pushed himself up from the mound.

'I hope my request hasn't offended you?' he asked anxiously.

'No,' I replied. 'I will promise you to repeat to my master all you have said. And I think you will find that men from the senate police will be there in the temple to prevent a riot.'

Gomer rushed to me and clasped my hands.

'Thank you,' he babbled. 'Thank you, sir. I knew when I first saw you as a young man ten years ago that you had a kind heart. "There," I said to myself, "there goes a really kind-hearted young man". Indeed I did.'

Gomer nodded his head solemnly. Then he looked dismayed.

'Not that you're no longer a young man,' he added hastily.

As I walked back to the villa, I wondered by what process of selection Caleb had chosen his disciples. A basket-maker, a shopkeeper, and a weaver – I knew the three men Gomer had named. On the surface they all seemed remarkably undistinguished, and Nathanael, the fisherman, seemed to have little to offer apart from his sinews. Ben was the only one of them who was really attractive. Gomer was the only one with some outside knowledge and a quick though crafty intelligence. Apart from their modest origins was there any quality these men had in common? Youth, I suppose, for none of them was older than thirty – with the exception of Gomer who must be nearly forty-five. Poverty? Manahem and Nathanael each owned a fishing-boat and came from quite well-to-do-families. It was then I remembered that out of the eight of them seven were unmarried. Being unmarried would certainly make it easier for them to leave home and follow Caleb. If so, why had Caleb chosen Ben who would surely have difficulty in leaving his wife to go to Jerusalem? As I opened the gate to the villa I recollected what Ben had told me of his first meeting with Caleb. Ben had stayed behind until Caleb had finished preaching in order to speak with him. Caleb, whose instinct was highly developed, must have recognized at once the honesty and trust-worthiness and loyalty of the stalwart young fisherman who stood before him. Perhaps in some curious way it was Ben who had chosen Caleb.

I found Joseph in the living-room.

'Though your face shows no trace of it,' he said as I came in, 'I feel sure you must be tired and thirsty after your excursion. So I have opened a bottle of the wine we found so pleasing earlier today.'

The bottle and wine-cups had been placed on the new table Manasseh had made. Joseph poured out the wine.

'Now let us sit down comfortably,' he said. 'For I want you to tell me every detail of what you have seen and heard.'

Joseph seemed unusually calm that evening as he sat in his favourite chair listening to all I had to tell him about Caleb and his followers. Nothing I said appeared to surprise him. He remained so unperturbed that I began to wonder if in his own mind he had not worked out every conceivable eventuality that might have occurred in regard to Caleb's actions and decisions. As we sipped the light red wine, I concluded by telling Joseph of Gomer's plea for protection.

'Yes,' Joseph said, as he rose to refill our cups. 'I shall certainly see to it that our senate police are alerted.'

I stared at Joseph. 'Do you mean that you are now resigned to Caleb going to Jerusalem?' I asked.

Joseph nodded. 'I have come to the conclusion that it is inevitable Caleb should do what he believes he must do,' he said.

I looked at Joseph in amazement.

'You will make no attempt to prevent him?' I asked.

'None,' Joseph answered. 'Because I can think of no method that would be effective.'

'I have never known you to give in so easily,' I said. 'Or have you thought out some alternative plan?'

Joseph was silent for a while. Then he slowly nodded his head.

'Yes, I suppose, in a way, I have,' Joseph replied. 'You see, during your absence, I came to the conclusion that even if Caleb were to stay here and to announce in this village that he was the Messiah, there would still be danger. The Romans must have spies here – as they have everywhere else – and the Sanhedrin also. The only way to protect Caleb from his fatal delusions is to persuade the powers in Jerusalem that Caleb is a mild and harmless madman. After all, men have arisen before now and proclaimed themselves the Messiah. It is not an unknown form of lunacy. Such delusions are surely more prevalent in our age than they have ever been. So this is now my intention. I shall write a report about Caleb and give it directly to the Head Council of the Sanhedrin. My report will condemn various blasphemous utterances Caleb has made. But at the same time I will make it clear that he is only a gentle and religious maniac. If I am the person from whom the members of the Sanhedrin learn about Caleb's pretensions, they will believe me. And no suspicion that I am trying for secret reasons to prevent a riot and save Caleb from condemnation to the cross will enter into their minds.'

Joseph drank his wine in silence.

'But, of course, for all this to be effective, I shall have to reach Jerusalem before Caleb,' he added. 'So I shall leave this house to-morrow.'

'If Caleb goes to Jerusalem, as now seems almost certain, and is treated as a harmless fanatic, what do you suppose will happen to him?' I asked.

'The crowds may throw stones at him. They may even use whips,' Joseph replied. 'But before Caleb has time to gain any following or to be taken seriously I shall arrange for him to be arrested and sent away from the city.'

'What if he returns?'

'He will not return,' Joseph said. 'For the shock will have made him realize that he is human. Caleb will most likely wander back to his father's vineyard. And neither you nor I will ever be troubled by him again.'

'It seems that our stay in Jerusalem will not be very peaceful,' I murmured.

Joseph took a small wafer of cake and began to eat it, chewing slowly and reflectively in the way I knew so well.

'It will not be "our stay", Raguel,' he said.

'No? Then why not?' I enquired.

'I think it better I should go alone,' Joseph answered.

I finished my wine and went to the table to refill my cup.

'Please can you tell me the reason?' I asked.

Joseph watched me carefully as if I were about to make some unexpected gesture.

'After you had left this afternoon I sat here thinking about you,' Joseph said. 'And suddenly it occurred to me that at times, for all your loyalty, you must have moods when you consider yourself almost a prisoner. You seldom leave this house. You rarely go out alone. You never take a journey without me. It may be quite possible that you seldom consciously imagine yourself a prisoner. But I am afraid the thought may lie there at the back of your mind. So I came to the conclusion that it would be wiser for you to spend two or three weeks on your own – without any responsibility. Travel to one of those villages high up in the mountains of the Lebanon. Do you remember how much we enjoyed the journey we made there together? Go wherever you like. But spend a few weeks on your own. I am sure it will do you good.'

I took a gulp of my wine. 'Is that the only reason you wish to go to Jerusalem alone?' I asked.

'No,' Joseph replied in his deep, calm voice. 'There is, of course, another reason, as you must appreciate since you now know of my plan. There are several people I shall have to meet in secret to report on Caleb. Another local leader will have to be found. In addition to that, I am certain to be invited to meet various politicians – and you know how much political discussions weary you. So from every point of view it is better I should be in Jerusalem alone.'

Joseph put down his wine-cup and smiled at me.

'I often wish I had been a poet or a writer,' he said with a sigh. 'For then I would have been a better companion for you, because you would have found my friends far more interesting. As it is, I can only offer you a release from the dullness of most of my acquaintances in Jerusalem by advising you to enjoy a pleasant rest in the Lebanon.'

I was observing Joseph steadily as he spoke. He seemed completely at ease and tranquil. I could not detect the slightest flicker of deceit. Moreover, I was glad in a way that I did not have to accompany him to the city, and I was thankful that within a few days' time it seemed almost certain that Caleb would no longer be present to disturb our friendship. Obviously, the quarrel which Joseph and I had endured earlier in the day was finished. When I returned from the Lebanon my relationship with Joseph would be warm and untroubled. Our lives would be serene once again.

I smiled back at Joseph. I lifted my cup of wine.

'Then let us drink to my journey,' I said.

I was honestly delighted that I would not have to face yet again living in Joseph's gaunt family house in Jerusalem.

CHAPTER FOUR

The outside appearance of my house in Jerusalem with its grey stone walls and heavy portico almost always depresses me, whereas the rooms inside never fail to please me. Over the years – and with Raguel's help – I have rid myself of the sombre furnishings in which my father delighted. I have acquired tapestries and carpets from Damascus, and beautifully gilded tables and chairs together with divans upholstered in brilliantly-coloured silks from Alexandria. The interior of the house is light and pleasant. I had brought Leah and Manasseh with me to supervise the other servants. Within a few hours I was comfortably ensconced; I had despatched my report to the High Council of the Sanhedrin; I had met three politicians of importance, and I had arranged to meet several more.

Late in the evening of the following day one of my agents came to inform me that Caleb, accompanied by eight of his disciples, had arrived in the city. They were staying at a small inn close to the Ephraim Gate.

Now, I had not lied to Raguel. But in a way I had been obliged to deceive him. I had belittled the danger of a riot; and I had avoided telling him of the risk that Caleb might possibly be condemned to death should I fail to convince the Sanhedrin he was an innocent lunatic. If Raguel had suspected there was any possibility I would become personally involved in trying to save Caleb from condemnation he would not have allowed me to come alone to the city.

Early the following morning I waited in my house. For once I was glad I lived so close to the temple. The courts and the arcades around it were daily used as a meeting-place; the large enclosed space served as a public forum. My agent had instructions to follow Caleb when he left the inn and to warn me as soon as he began to move in the direction of the temple. I was almost certain that Caleb and his disciples would soon appear.

I was ready. And the instant my agent arrived I left the house. It was early in the day, but the outer courts of the temple were already full of people. The work on the new edifice which had begun forty years previously was now nearing completion. More elaborate and larger than the two former temples, the building was considered one of the most splendid and beautiful of our day. It was unfortunate that corrupt temple-priests had allowed the arcades to be infested by merchants. Admittedly stalls were needed for the animals offered for sacrifices. Cages were required for the doves. Offices equipped with tables and coffers were used by the money-changers who in their turn were necessary because pilgrims came from foreign lands with foreign money, and coins stamped with any image were not accepted by the merchants who sold the sacrificial animals. This was all part of the temple-priests' fraud; for only our own currency was held to be valid. But all this paraphernalia of shops and exchange-counters and cattle-markets which reminded one of some bazaar should never have been allowed inside the temple precincts. It was vulgar and irreligious. But a far worse sacrilege in my eyes was the south-eastern tower of the Castle which stood above the temple. In this fortress were stationed the Roman officers and soldiers who kept us in subjugation. I had been inside and seen the huge living-quarters. With lofty, spacious halls and galleries and well-appointed baths, the Roman barracks were more like a palace than a castle. A broad flight of stairs led down into the temple grounds. Down those stairs could descend the centurions and their men if there were any riot or insurrection.

I found Caleb standing in a corner of the Court of the Gentiles which was open to everyone. He was surrounded by his disciples. Already a small crowd had gathered to hear him speak; the people had been attracted, I was sure, by his unusual and youthful appearance. That morning Caleb looked even more handsome and serene than when I had previously seen him, but beneath his serenity I could now glimpse a trace of almost fatalistic despair. And in some intuitive way, as he preached in a harmless manner about the need to believe that the Kingdom of God was very near, I could sense what he was thinking. In his mind lay the thought:' I know I must suffer. But I dread the moment when they will touch me.'

I made sure that the chief of the senate police who had been alerted was present. Then I stood at the very back of the crowd, in the shadow of a thick column, and listened to what Caleb was saying.

'Therefore you must not let yourselves be concerned with mundane anxieties,' he was saying. 'You must sacrifice no particle of your spirit for the sake of material gain. You must not risk losing your soul for the sake of pompous earthly glory or of envied seats of honour. I tell you that when the Kingdom of God comes, it is those who are simple and poor who will be the first to drink the wine of heaven. You have no enemies before God except your own selves. It is your passions that cut you off from God.'

All this was innocuous. It was the kind of stuff people in the city would expect from a country preacher. I even began to hope and presently to pray with fervour that Caleb had changed his mind about his proclamation. The throng around him was growing larger – probably because of the strangely attractive personality which emanated from him.

'But all of us must be careful we do not blame our neighbours,' Caleb continued. 'We have seen the money-changers here beneath the arcades of this temple, within its holy precincts. We have all seen their eagerness as they greedily shuffle the coins across their counters, grasping at each piece of silver as though it were the bread of life. We may think, when we watch their frantic scrabblings and endless efforts, that the money-changers have lost their souls. But can we blame them? No, I tell you. We can no more blame them for losing their souls than we can blame a withered orange-tree for not bearing

93

fruit. Bless the money-changers, I say. Bless them in compassion for the misery of their spirits.'

There were murmurs among the crowd. The slightest criticism of the money-changers implied a criticism of the temple-priests who it was well known had a share in their profits.

'Why should we despise the money-changers, shopkeepers and merchants – and yet admire the Pharisees who encourage the presence of all these tradesmen in the temple precincts and gain dishonest wealth thereby?' Caleb demanded suddenly. 'Do we respect the Pharisees because their robes are immaculate? Because they wash their hands a dozen times a day? Because they receive salutations as they strut across the market-place? Because they occupy the seats of honour? Surely that would be foolish, for what does their outward appearance matter? Does God care where they sit in our synagogues? No, I tell you. God is concerned only with the spirit. And if we were to look within the souls of most Pharisees what would we discover? What indeed! Hypocrisy, certainly. Envy or greed, probably. Or perhaps a mere nothingness – an empty void. Pity them, I tell you. Weep for the Pharisees, if you will – with all their elaborate rituals and clever figures of speech. Weep for the proud hypocrites, those shameless dissemblers who dare to despise the humble and the poor. Weep in your compassion. But do not admire them. For they are mere baubles set on a huckster's stall, mere straw on a stable's floor. Even so, I tell you, even so God will have mercy on them and will bless them. For God's mercy is infinite.'

A crowd is like a herd of animals, for an impulse at one extremity of it is reproduced at the other. And while Caleb had spoken, the section of the crowd in which some of the Pharisees were standing had begun first to stir, and then to mutter, and soon to growl with a quiet yet menacing indignation. Presently the whole crowd seemed to shudder and heave in resentment.

'Who are you to speak with such authority?' a voice called out. 'Who are you to *dare* to decide whom God will bless? Who *are* you?'

I could feel my heart pounding in my chest. I looked towards Caleb. He was standing motionless. His face seemed very pale. Then he swallowed.

'My name is Caleb,' he said. And I could see and almost hear Gomer's sigh of relief.

'But who *are* you?' the voice shouted. 'Who gave you the right to use God's name? Go on. Tell us. By what authority do you have the impudence to speak of the blessing of the Lord, our God?'

Caleb's face was now so white I thought he would faint. Once again – perhaps because I felt so close to him – I knew what he was about to say. I knew that the words he would now pronounce would convict him utterly. And there was nothing I could do to stop it, for as yet he had said nothing to justify his arrest. Caleb took in a deep breath. Then he flung out his right arm. At that instant I was certain that the terrible moment had come – the moment that nothing in the world could have prevented.

'I have the right,' Caleb cried out. 'I have the authority. For I am the Teacher of Righteousness. I am indeed the Long-awaited One. I am the Son of David, I tell you. I am the King of Israel who the prophets foretold would save this nation and would redeem mankind. I am the Messiah.'

For an instant there was complete silence. Then a low roar of fury came from the crowd, and it began to move, pressing against the disciples who had formed a half-circle round Caleb. Now the crowd bellowed like a wounded beast, thrashing in frenzy. Then it began to snarl in horrible spasms of hatred, lurching forward in an ecstasy of violence. At that moment it was certainly the speed of the senate police which saved Caleb's life – and the lives of his disciples as well. For as soon as Caleb had begun speaking, I had made a sign to the chief of police. Rapidly, he and his men broke a way through the crowd, lashing out with their staves. Reinforcements followed. Quickly with their staves the men formed a barrier of defence around Caleb and the disciples.

'Disperse!' the chief called out. 'Disperse – and go back to your homes.'

The crowd murmured in displeasure but was still. The chief pointed to Caleb.

'I am arresting this man,' he shouted in his loud, raucous voice. 'If anyone impedes that arrest he will suffer.'

Then the chief glanced up at the Castle, towering above us.

'If I am prevented from carrying out my duty, I will summon the aid of a centurion and his men,' he told the crowd. 'And you know what that will mean,' he added. 'Disperse, at once, I order you.'

The crowd hesitated. But already some of the Pharisees had begun to move away. The animal-like entity of the crowd was beginning to disintegrate. The chief's men pushed aside the disciples and seized hold of Caleb. I saw him shudder as they clutched his arms and shoulders. His unconscious response to their touching him reminded me of the dove in our garden, the dove with the broken leg. But at present there was no Simon who could soothe Caleb's desperate efforts to free himself. Some of the chief's men now formed an alley with their staves through which Caleb was dragged away.

I did not wish to meet any of the disciples – not even Ben – for it was essential that at no stage should I be publicly associated with them. I hurried back home. At least the first part of my plan to save Caleb and to prevent a widespread riot had succeeded. And there was a meeting of the Sanhedrin that afternoon.

The art of politics and of life itself, come to that, lies in foreseeing every possible eventuality and preparing for it. But Caleb that morning had ruffled the smoothness of my plan. When he began to speak, I had not expected him to give the impression of such calmness and deliberation. His cool manner and immaculate appearance at the outset of his speech, combined with the authority of his tone and the sincerity of his utterances, would now make it very difficult for me to convince the Sanhedrin that Caleb was a harmless young madman of little consequence. Moreover, his remarks about the money-changers had annoyed the priests, and his attack on the Pharisees had enraged not only the pedants among them but the whole nobility. I would now have many enemies at the meeting.

And so it proved.

As soon as I entered the high-ceilinged Council Chamber I sensed animosity. Caleb's arrest was the first matter to be discussed. Since I was the only member who had met Caleb I was asked to speak. I now repeated openly to the senate the gist of my secret report to the Council. I said that I had heard of various wild remarks that a young preacher had made in the village where I lived on the shore of the Lake of Tiberias. I told them I had summoned the man to my house and interrogated him. I said I had concluded that though some of his statements could be considered blasphemous, the man was ignorant and politically harmless. He was no more dangerous than hundreds of mendicants and self-styled prophets who roamed the countryside of our land. Caleb was obviously deluded and probably insane. I ended by saying that I had been appalled that morning by his blasphemy in the temple, and I proposed that he should be expelled from the city immediately.

The High Priest, Caiaphas, smoothed down his robes as he stood up.

'It appears that this Caleb has been at large in the district of Galilee for some time,' he began. 'May we ask why you did not report on his activities sooner?'

I bowed in respect to his rank before I replied. 'Because I met him only this last week,' I said.

He nodded. Caiaphas had reached his position of distinction only two years previously, yet already he had assumed a kind of tired dignity in his middle-age. Over the years, I felt sure, he had trained each line of his face, each feature, to express a certain worn piety and resignation. The result was impressive. Perhaps he practised his expression each morning in front of a looking-glass.

'May we enquire what decided you – as you stated in your report – to invite the young man to visit you in your house?' he asked.

I understood perfectly well the suggestion which lay behind his question – and so must many others who were present.

'I am grateful to the High Priest for his question,' I answered with a pleasant smile, as Caiaphas lowered himself into his seat. 'I am grateful because it gives me the opportunity to address this noble assembly on a matter I consider most important. We of the Sanhedrin form the senate of this country. Admittedly, as a result of our deliberations in most cases we can only *recommend* a course of action to a higher authority. Nevertheless we wield great power. Now, most of us live here in our holy city. Few of us reside in the country villages. So there must – and I say this in all humility – there must inevitably exist a danger that we should be out of touch with the ordinary country people of our land.'

I paused and gazed steadily around the assembly.

'I am fortunate inasmuch as I live both in the city and in the country,' I told them. 'I know town people, and I know countryfolk. And there is a difference between them. Labourers in the field and villagers are at once simpler than we might suppose – and more imaginative. They believe devoutly in the Lord, our God. They are deeply patriotic. They respect this assembly. But part of their mind dwells in a region which lies beyond the soil they till. They are fanciful – and often deluded in their fantasies. They believe in weird spirits and demons. Their imagination is so intense they can even hear voices. Sometimes they are even so deluded as to believe that God, the God of Israel, speaks to them in person.'

Once again I paused in order to gain the effect I required.

'This Caleb whom some of you saw and heard this morning is such a person,' I stated. As I spoke, I glanced quickly around the assembly. Immediately I sensed that, so far, the majority was still hostile to me, so I must be careful not to give the impression I had any personal interest in Caleb.

'In his vain delusion,' I continued, 'Caleb has spoken to me of a voice which he believes to be the very voice of God. In the presence of my secretary and even in the presence of my house-servants he has babbled to me of this voice which he claims has told him he is one of the Prophets. And later during the morning that he came to see me, he became so intoxicated by his fancies that at one moment it almost seemed he believed himself to be the Anointed One for whose coming we have awaited so long. He even announced he would travel to Jerusalem. I cannot state that Caleb actually claimed to be the Messiah, for my revulsion at his pretensions was violent – even though I knew I was listening to a madman. Perhaps you will blame me. Perhaps you will think I should have listened to this deluded man's insane ravings to the very end. But I could not. For my disgust overcame me. And I gave orders for Caleb to be thrown out of my house.'

As I concluded this sentence, there were murmurs of approval. The High Priest retained his expression of careworn piety.

'The very next day I wrote out a report on the behaviour of Caleb,' I continued. 'The following day I set out for Jerusalem. As soon as I reached the city I sent my report to the Head Council of this assembly, as you all now know. I also alerted our police in case of a riot. I am sure you will appreciate that I could have done no more. And now this poor deluded preacher has declared himself to be the Messiah – within the very precincts of our holy temple. Accordingly, what course of action should we take? What should we do? What punishment should we inflict on him? Have Caleb stoned to death for his impiety? Recommend that he should be crucified? I confess I am not certain. All of you know the old saying that one must beware of throwing out the good with the bad. In this case I think the dictum may well apply. I have already told you of the devoutness and patriotism of our countryfolk. Am I being sacrilegious or am I in my turn being fanciful if I suggest that one day – one day soon, we all of us hope and pray daily – the Son of David may be born in a country village? Is that beyond the bounds of possibility? I am convinced it is not, for we all know that nothing – nothing on earth or in heaven – is beyond the bounds of the Divine Will of God. And now that my anger and distrust at Caleb's pretensions have subsided, now that I can contemplate this vain and impious preacher with a degree of detachment, I am beginning to wonder if Caleb's pretensions are anything more than a distortion – a vile distortion, I admit – yet nevertheless no more than a distortion of that highly-developed imagination of the people about whom I have spoken. Caleb's ravings are certainly bad. But I claim that the popular imagination is good. For I believe with all my soul that it is in the soil of that simple, honest and infinitely devout imagination that our Messiah may be born. And have not our holy Prophets foretold it? Am I pronouncing any new thought? On the contrary. We have been led to believe that the Messiah will be born in a poor home in a poor village. And I am convinced he will be nurtured and eventually welcomed in the soil of devoutness and popular idealism. Kill Caleb in the badness of his insanity, and you will kill the spirit of the people's imagination in all its goodness. For remember this. In their honest simplicity the people of Galilee believed – and still believe – in Caleb's preaching. God has told us through his holy Prophets that our minds and hearts must be prepared to receive the Messiah. Crucify Caleb, and you may delay – at least for our lifetime – the coming of the Son of God.'

I sat down. There was an intense silence. They all remained perfectly still. Then Caiaphas began to gather together his robes with hands that trembled. His look of piety had gone. His face was swollen with indignation. But so elaborate were his preparations to rise to his feet that Jotham had stood up before him and was commanding by his strong presence the complete attention of the assembly.

I scarcely knew Jotham. Though I admired his integrity, I found the impeccable and constant uprightness of Jotham's character slightly depressing. If only – I could not resist thinking – if only he would sin just once then I would be assured he was human. However, there was no hypocrisy about him. His life was plain for all of us to inspect. And there he stood before us, a grey-haired, resolute man of about sixty, carefully dressed, moderate in his views and speech, respectable both in his public life as a lawyer and in his private life with his deeply religious wife and his five children, as fastidious in his morals as in his choice of dress, and, above all, eminently just. So well known was Jotham for the justness of his views that I felt certain the fate of Caleb depended on the attitude Jotham would take.

'We have listened most attentively to the speech of our noble friend,' he began in his clear, dry voice. 'And we are grateful to him.'

In his seat of honour, Caiaphas fluttered his robes with annoyance.

'Grateful?' he muttered. 'Grateful for what? Grateful to him for condoning blasphemy?'

'We are grateful to him,' Jotham continued steadily, 'if only because he has reminded us here in this assembly that although we are not chosen by the people, we of this senate represent – or at least should represent – the people of our nation. And it is, if I may say so, of extreme importance that we should remember this fact when we are considering what punishment should be meted out to any man such as Caleb – a man who in public has blasphemed against our God and who in public has uttered words of treason against authority.'

When Jotham used the term 'treason' I was immediately afraid of the drift of logic his argument might take.

'For blasphemy, the penalty is stoning. For treason, it is crucifixion,' Jotham stated with an odd tremor in his voice. 'But our friend has warned us that we must be very careful before we impose or recommend either sentence. He has presented most eloquently the reasons why Caleb – this Caleb, I may add, of whose name and identity most of us have only heard this morning – should be acquitted. His discourse was so fluent that I, for one, could not help wishing we could have the advantage of hearing his voice more frequently in this assembly.'

When Jotham paused I was almost certain he was about to change the course of his address.

'As we all did, I listened most assiduously to our friend's inferences and conclusions,' Jotham announced. 'But I must confess I could not follow the chain of his reasoning. Please let our friend correct me if I am mistaken, but I apprehend the logic of his discourse to be as follows. Our countryfolk are simple, devout and highly imaginative. The Son of David will, in the mercy of Almighty God, one day be born in a simple village. The country-people of Galilee believe in the preachings of Caleb. Therefore if we condemn Caleb, we will offend the popular idealism and disturb the ground in which the Saviour of our race will be born. Am I correct?'

Jotham turned his thin, impassive face towards me in enquiry. I was silent. Anything I now said would only expose the speciousness of my argument which I had hoped in my vanity to conceal.

'Am I correct?' Jotham repeated.

In silence I nodded my head.

'Then I have two observations to make,' Jotham said. 'And I will state them as shortly as I can, for I am aware there are several members present here this afternoon who are probably better qualified than I am to speak. My first observation is that our friend has made no attempt to refute the crimes of blasphemy and treason Caleb has committed. How can he? The facts are clear and undisputed. He has only proclaimed his own personal view that Caleb is insane and must be expelled from this city – perhaps, I presume, to be detained in some place as a lunatic. Now, I must tell you that I myself happened to be in the Court of the Gentiles in the temple this morning. I saw Caleb, and I heard him preach. And I am afraid I must differ from our friend in his conclusion. If ever in my life I saw a man in complete possession of his thoughts and of his words it was Caleb.'

Jotham paused – not for effect but to allow the murmurs of approval which had greeted his last remark to subside.

'My second observation is this,' Jotham continued. 'Our friend's main plea for Caleb's acquittal lies not in his guilt or innocence, but in a more general argument about popular idealism. "Kill Caleb," he told us, "and you will kill the spirit of the people." Now, I must beg to disagree with this statement most profoundly. The spirit of the people does not reside in superstitions and false prophecies. It does not depend on being nurtured by unsound dogmas and unwarranted attacks on the leaders of this nation. The spirit of our people exists and depends on the truth of the Holy Laws of God which have been handed down to us from generation to generation. The spirit of our nation resides in the Holiness of Truth, not in fantasies. Our spirit is our Faith. And therefore any man who blasphemes against our Faith offends our spirit.'

Once again Jotham was obliged to pause, while the assembly expressed its approbation of his sentiments.

'We have been reminded we have a duty as representatives of the nation,' he continued. 'Indeed, this is true. But I need not remind you all of our other obligations. In our hearts we know we are responsible to the Procurator, our Governor, Valerius Gratus. And how, may I ask, how can we possibly discharge our responsibility to our Governor if we acquit a man who has publicly declared himself to be the King of Israel? A man who has nearly caused a violent riot? A man who has publicly committed an act of treason against the Roman Emperor whom the Governor represents?'

Jotham raised his hand for silence.

'I will end briefly,' he said. 'I maintain that Caleb has offended against the spirit of our people. He has committed treason against the Emperor. He has committed blasphemy against the name of the Lord, our God who has made us his Chosen People.'

As Jotham surveyed the assembly, for the first time he showed a slight trace of emotion, and his lips quivered.

'In our capacity of guardians of the nation under the aegis of Valerius Gratus,' he concluded, 'we cannot escape our responsibility. I am certain the only honest course of action open to us is to recommend that Caleb should be crucified – and to leave it to the Governor's judgment and discretion as to whether the sentence should be carried out.'

As Jotham ended his speech I rose quietly to my feet. When the applause began, I bowed to Jotham, then to the High Priest who was already rising to speak, and lastly to the assembly in general. Then I left the chamber.

The result of the debate was now certain. Therefore it was essential that I should be the first person to approach Valerius Gratus. So I hastened westward across the city to the Palace.

In his heart, I am certain that Valerius Gratus considered the Jews a difficult and stubborn people. His wide-ranging mind was affronted by the concentrated intensity of our religion; his sensibility was outraged by the severity of our rites in general, and by the practice of circumcision in particular. But he was one of those men who believed that wealth – if considerable – overcame the barriers of class and of race. The possession of riches made, in his eyes, brothers of all men; affluence atoned for the colour of a skin that deviated from white; opulence made up for uncouth practices; command of money expiated outlandish rites. And although my wealth lay mainly in my country properties, if judged by the standards of my nation I was a rich man. For my part, I despised Valerius Gratus for being the servile instrument of a corrupt and tyrannical Empire.

On this mutual basis of disapproval the two of us had met – and to our joint astonishment had become friends. I found it infinitely easier to converse with him about art and history and philosophy than with my fellow-members of the Sanhedrin. Valerius Gratus, for his part, may have found me less disputatious and bigoted – and perhaps more cultured – than most of my countrymen. Moreover, his wife, a charming and unusually intelligent woman, had taken a liking to me. During the five years he had been Governor I had visited the Palace whenever I was in Jerusalem. His spies and informers must certainly have acquainted him with my predilections – which, after all, accorded with the foibles of his Emperor. But this information did not appear to have changed his attitude towards me.

I could now see the tall white marble walls of the Palace, glittering in the sun. The centurion in charge of the Imperial guards at the gate recognized me and saluted. I entered the wide, spacious courtyard with an unpleasant trepidation. I could not rid my mind of the vision of Caleb being dragged away to the prison, trembling and struggling frantically to escape – like the dove I had found by the stream. By now I had realized that the incident of the dove had assumed the importance of a permanent obsession in my mind.

A secretary escorted me to an anteroom. A short while later I was shown into the Audience Chamber. As I entered, Valerius Gratus rose from his gilt throne and advanced to greet me. He was an impressive-looking man of medium height, inclined to stoutness with a smooth plump face which was extraordinarily white and which in repose was so motionless and still that one could well imagine he had already been transformed into the marble statue which would certainly be erected in his memory if his ambition were fulfilled.

'I am delighted to see you, Joseph,' he said. 'But I must confess I am surprised. First, I did not know you had returned to Jerusalem. Secondly, if you *were* in the city I supposed that you would be attending the meeting of the Sanhedrin this afternoon.'

'Excellency,' I began – for I was always careful to observe a formal distance between us, 'Excellency,' I said, 'I *did* attend, but I left the meeting.'

His slightly glazed brown eyes examined me carefully.

'Has anything unfortunate occurred?' he asked.

I smiled grimly. 'Not to *me*, Excellency,' I replied.

'I am pleased to hear you reassure me,' he said. He pointed to two comfortable chairs at the end of the room. 'Let us sit down and talk for a while,' he continued. 'You must forgive me if I am unable to enjoy your company for long. But I have a meeting with a legate from Egypt this evening.'

As we crossed the lofty hall, I observed the ivory and gold inlays of the furniture. Such is the divided nature of the human mind that even though I was concentrating deeply on the words I would shortly employ, I could not help registering the trivial fact that the quality of the gilt tables was inferior to my own. Sometimes I think that if I were about to be slain by robbers I would be concerned if my hair were disarranged.

'I am listening,' the Governor announced in his pleasant, cultured voice as we sat down.

Briefly I told him that in Galilee I had met a young, enthusiastic but demented preacher called Caleb.

'In the temple this morning, Excellency, as I am sure you will have heard,' I continued, 'Caleb announced that he was the King of Israel and the long-expected Messiah. His treason and blasphemy nearly caused a riot.'

Valerius Gratus joined the tips of his plump fingers together and contemplated them.

'So I was informed,' he murmured.

'When I left the meeting of the Sanhedrin this afternoon,' I told him, 'Jotham had just finished a fine speech in which he said that Caleb had committed treason and therefore the Sanhedrin should recommend to you, as Governor, that Caleb should be crucified, leaving it to your discretion as to whether the sentence should be carried out. There is no doubt in my mind that Jotham's speech will convince the whole assembly.'

Valerius Gratus glanced up at me, then resumed his examination of his fingertips.

'The Sanhedrin is an unusually intelligent body of men,' he commented, speaking half-aloud. 'They defer to my authority as Procurator – or Governor, as you Jews prefer to call it. And if I decide to execute the sentence, the whole odium of crucifying a bereft young man will fall on me personally.'

The Governor paused and gazed straight into my eyes.

'I think you did mention that he was a young man?' he enquired.

'Yes, Excellency.'

'And I would presume that since this young man is reputed to have gained a considerable following in Galilee,' he continued, 'this Caleb of yours must be endowed not only with eloquence but with charm of manner and perhaps beauty of person?'

I understood at once what he was suggesting. I smiled as my eyes met his gaze.

'Yes, Excellency,' I answered. 'I would suppose that his appearance has contributed to such success as he has gained. As to his charm, I fear I am no judge, for I have met Caleb only on one occasion.'

'Only on one occasion,' Valerius Gratus repeated. 'And what impression did you form of the young man's character?'

'He is ardent to convince, yet devoid of any political acumen,' I said. 'He sometimes has flashes of intuition that lend him wisdom in matters of the spirit, but he is almost wholly ignorant of matters concerning the everyday world. Most important of all, he is – to use the apt word your Excellency employed – Caleb is essentially "bereft". He is an innocent who should never have left Galilee.'

'And do I gather that in your view this innocent should be acquitted?' the Governor enquired.

'If your Excellency will permit me to use forceful words, then I would say "Yes, most certainly. It would be an act of injustice were he to be killed".'

Valerius Gratus was watching me steadily, his face immobile.

'Yet by all accounts Jotham is an honourable and fair-minded man,' he said. 'Why, then, should he recommend that Caleb should be put to death?'

I was ready for this question; I had been expecting it.

'First, because, although he is just, Jotham tends to be narrow-minded, like so many lawyers,' I answered. 'His susceptibilities have been affronted by Caleb's words of treason and blasphemy. Secondly, I must confess that when I heard Caleb preach this morning, I realized that between his fits of insanity there are lucid periods when any person who was hearing him for the first time would suppose that Caleb was in his right mind.'

'But you know better?'

'I do indeed.'

'And you tried to persuade the Sanhedrin of Caleb's lunacy and innocence?'

'Yes, Excellency,' I replied. 'I spoke before Jotham did.'

'But you failed to convince them?'

'Indeed. Completely.'

'Why?'

'Because many of the Pharisees present had heard Caleb in the temple this morning. And they had been outraged by his attack on them.'

'You inform me that Caleb declared himself "King of Israel". I have heard this from other sources. Was his statement direct and unequivocal?'

'Yes.'

'There could have been no misunderstanding or misreporting of his words?'

I understood the gentle hint.

'There is no doubt that Caleb uttered the words,' I answered. 'I heard them, and so did many other witnesses of considerable repute. But I took the phrase in a spiritual rather than in a temporal sense. It was indeed as a symbolic rather than as a factual declaration.'

'But Caleb employed the phrases "I am the Son of David. I am the King of Israel"?'

'Yes,' I replied.

Valerius Gratus sighed.

'I am sure you must appreciate the difficulty of my position,' he said. 'For you must be aware of the intense fanaticism of your people. Caleb, this morning, not only committed an act of treason against the Emperor, but an act of blasphemy against your God. I am not so stupid as to believe that a near riot was caused merely because of Caleb's treason. It was his declaration that he was the Messiah which incensed the mob. So consider my position. The whole populace by now has heard of Caleb's words. The people are enraged by his blasphemy. The Pharisees are still further angered by his criticism of their way of life. Therefore, if I acquit Caleb I incur the hatred of the people and the hostility of the Pharisees.'

Valerius Gratus parted his hands and raised them with a graceful gesture into the air, and then let them fall on to his gold-encrusted robe.

'But there is a worse danger,' he continued. 'As you may imagine, although I have many powerful friends in Rome, I have – like most men in my position – a few enemies in high places, and they are waiting patiently for me to make a mistake. The news of this morning's disturbance will certainly be reported to the Legate of Syria. In his turn, he will mention it in his usual despatch to Rome. Now, suppose that I acquit Caleb and let him go free? What then? Some enemy of mine has only to approach the Emperor and say: "A dangerous fanatic in the province of Judea publicly pronounced himself, in the temple of Jerusalem, to be the King of Israel. The Jewish Sanhedrin recommended that he should be crucified. But even though this dangerous fanatic had committed an act of outrageous treason against your title and your authority – even so – your own Procurator acquitted the criminal and set him free." And if that were said to the Emperor, *then* what would be the result?'

Valerius Gratus was silent. His noble, impassive face was turned towards me, and the light from the window illumined his motionless features. As he sat there, stolid in thought, suddenly a twitch of nerves shook him in a violent spasm. His neck twisted, and his mouth and cheeks were distorted and thus remained for a quick moment, askew and misshapen. I stared in horror. For in front of my very eyes the polished marble bust I had beheld was now split open and disintegrated in a shudder of fear. Swiftly his hands covered the cracked and deformed face. An instant later, Valerius Gratus dropped his hands. The convulsion was over. The marble image had been conjoined once again without any sign of a fracture. And the Procurator of Judea was contemplating me with dispassion.

'I have not met Caleb,' he said. 'I do not intend to meet him. In my five years as Procurator I have gained sufficient experience of your people to avoid affording them the satisfaction of vulgar demonstrations in front of this Palace. So I will not allow the council of the Sanhedrin to bring Caleb before me for condemnation. If a recommendation reaches me that Caleb should be crucified for treason, I am afraid I must tell you that only one course is open to me. That course is to confirm the sentence and to make certain that Caleb is crucified. I shall also give instructions to my centurions to assure that the people should be restrained from any manifestation – either in the man's favour or against him.'

Valerius Gratus rose to his feet, and I followed his action. Obviously my audience was at an end. Slowly we walked together out of the long room. As we approached the heavy double-doors which led to the head of the stairs, the Governor stopped.

'I am sorry that I must disappoint you, Joseph,' he said.

'Perhaps your Excellency may yet see a way of displaying clemency,' I replied, mumbling my words in the vexation of my failure.

'No,' he answered. 'Definitely no.'

'At least may I thank you for listening to me,' I said.

For an instant Valerius Gratus touched my shoulder, then removed his hand.

'When this unfortunate matter is concluded, I hope and trust you will come and see me again,' he told me.

'If I may – most certainly I will,' I replied.

He began to move, then came to a halt once more.

'You know, Joseph, it is a lonely existence that my wife and I lead here in Palestine,' he said. 'We have tried to overcome the barriers of prejudice against us – but without much success. You, Joseph, are one of the very few Jews with whom we can discourse with any degree of mutual understanding. And we know perfectly well that as a patriot you would be pleased to see the Roman forces of occupation removed, and the two of us with them – and please do not bother to deny it.'

He paused and stared at me in silence for a while.

'I have many worries,' he added. 'I have to govern a most intractable people. However, at least I can take comfort in the loyalty of my Roman officers.'

He was standing very still. His glazed brown eyes were concentrated on my face.

'But even in that respect I am not free from concern,' he said. 'Many of my centurions are married and have families, and although in your position you would never have noticed the fact, the truth is that on the stipend of a centurion it is quite expensive to live in Jerusalem.'

The brown eyes gazed at me steadily, without blinking. The statue was wholly restored. Each lineament was carved solidly and confronted me with ponderous authority.

'In fact,' Valerius Gratus continued, 'I fear that my centurions may sometimes find themselves almost impoverished.'

His gaze was still fixed on me, but an odd light now seemed to be reflected in the eyes of the statue.

'However, I must not inflict my own worries on you,' the Governor concluded. 'I am sure that you have your own private affairs to resolve.'

Again he touched my shoulder.

'It has been pleasant to see you, Joseph,' he said. 'Let us meet when this sorry matter no longer oppresses us.'

Then the Governor turned away and walked slowly back towards his throne.

As I walked out of the Palace, I reflected that Valerius Gratus was fast learning the art of politics and was practising it quite subtly.

Late that afternoon the Sanhedrin sent a recommendation to the Palace that Caleb should be crucified. The next morning the Procurator confirmed the sentence.

Once authority has been invoked, and once the invocation has been satisfied, events turn with the smoothness of a heavy wheel on a well-oiled axis. Authority has given the wheel its momentum, and it appears to revolve inexorably. The following afternoon Caleb was taken out of prison and scourged publicly by Roman soldiers. I learned this from Manasseh in the solitude of my house which I never left all day. That evening, after enduring his lashes and the insults of the mob with a fortitude that surprised many of the onlookers, Caleb was taken back to prison. By a strong effort of will I was able to prevent myself from dwelling too intensely on these events – though horrible images of the laceration of the smooth olive skin of Caleb's body seared my mind. But I knew I must keep a firm control over my emotions. For I was now the only person who could save Caleb from death.

The next afternoon I was visiting various places on the other side of the city, so I did not see the crowds who surrounded the exhausted, pitiably torn body of the young man as he staggered forward under the weight of his cross, toiling northward along the narrow alleys that led towards the hill outside the walls.

For once in my life the ambition of my spirit coincided with the passion of my heart. The wheel of authority might turn relentlessly. But by now my new plan was prepared. Caleb would not die as young Simon had died. Besides, there were political reasons why Caleb should live.

It was not until late in the afternoon of the following day that my plan forced me to face the anguish of visiting the hill. I had not been to that place of horror, that evil, barren patch of ground, rounded and bare like a dead man's skull; I had not even approached it since the occasion when my father had dragged me up the incline to behold Simon.

Several people were kneeling there. I recognized my servants Leah and Manasseh, and, crouched behind them, was the little kitchen-maid called Merab. I noticed Ben and Gomer, who were also deep in prayer. The other disciples must have fled from the city. The declining rays of a pale sun, obscured by a light mist, illuminated the bald crest of the hill.

And Caleb was hanging on the cross, his scarred body motionless, his eyes closed in a merciful swoon.

PART THREE

CHAPTER ONE

Oh God, I do trust in you. Your servant, Ben, trusts in you. I am just a fisherman from the lake, but I can warrant I have more faith than any double-faced Pharisee from the city. In fact, all of us in Galilee trust in you. And, what is more, we still believe that Caleb is the Messiah whom you have sent to save your chosen people. We believe he is your son, oh God. We understand why he had to come to Jerusalem and be condemned – because he told us the reason. He told Gomer and me and those other disciples the day before we left the lake. We knew he must be whipped and crucified. We knew that all the things the prophets had foretold must happen. But please God, dear God, do not let him suffer for so long.

And where is the band of women of Jerusalem whose hearts you touched so that they visit the cross of each victim and hand up to him a sponge soaked in wine at the end of a stick to alleviate his suffering? Why are they not here this afternoon? Why cannot Leah or Manasseh go and fetch wine? Why doesn't Joseph *order* them to bring wine? I can't understand it. What is the use of them kneeling, lost in their prayer, when they could do something to spare him suffering? Neither Gomer nor I can go through the city walls to buy wine for fear of being recognized.

Dear God, surely Caleb has suffered enough already for the prophecy to come true? Or is it because of us disciples that he is suffering for so many hours on the cross? Is it because we failed him? Is he suffering for our guilt? If so, dear God, let *us* be punished – not him. At any rate, let *me* be punished. For I must confess my sins and weakness.

When I saw the chief of police and his men coming into the court of the temple to arrest Caleb, I was scared. Oh God, I admit it. I only stood firm because I was too frightened to move. Then I saw them grasp hold of Caleb, and rage made me brave for a moment, because I thought, 'How dare they maul him about, those paid ignorant fools, when Caleb wouldn't even let us touch his hand?' But I still couldn't find the courage to move. And in silence and hopelessness I watched them drag him away. At the moment of his arrest the eight of us were in danger of our lives. If the police had not protected us I honestly believe the crowds might have torn us to pieces. Nathanael is still hiding in the city in the house of some relation. The rest of them – apart from Gomer here – have fled back to Galilee, or so I have heard. *Their* belief can't have been very deep. But I mustn't start priding myself on my own behaviour – or I'll get hypocritical like the Pharisees he told us about.

After Caleb had been taken off to prison, I began to have my doubts. I must confess it. I was disloyal in my mind, and I was stupid. I couldn't help wondering if I had done right to leave Galilee and come to the city. After all, my father was most upset. He even had to hire a complete stranger to take my place in the boat. And Rachel, of course, was furious. In fact, she was so angry that she left the house the evening I broke the news to her, and went to stay with her mother. Well, she's never done *that* before. 'Ben' she said, 'you'll regret this day so long as you live.' So I was really worried, and when Caleb was imprisoned I couldn't help wondering if it hadn't all been a mistake. I know it was wrong of me. I was plain weak. But now that I have seen Caleb's courage, I believe again. Forgive me for my time of doubt. And please forgive me my other sins. Let me confess them to you, oh God. Let me confess . . .

Before I married Rachel, I broke one of the commandments. In fact, I broke the commandment quite often. I was very young. I wasn't clever. I wasn't even good at my job. I was clumsy in the boat. I hadn't yet learnt the knack of handling a net. In those days my father was very poor. The fishing was none too good. We often went hungry. There didn't seem much to enjoy in life. But I had strength, and I was well made – I could see it in their eyes when the women looked at me. Sometimes they'd jokingly put a hand on my shoulder or ruffle my hair, and then I would feel the warm glow rising in me. And I liked it. I liked it so much that after a time I lost control of myself somehow. And I did wrong. Very wrong. I committed my first real sin. That was bad enough, I know full well. But it was only the beginning. Presently, I started going with one girl after another. Soon I was having a woman almost every night. And so it went on – because I could see it was giving them pleasure, and it gave me pleasure as well,

I do admit. In fact, now I come to look back, it often gave me a very great deal of pleasure indeed. I felt I was making use of the one single blessing I had really got in life.

But then one evening I met Rachel. I had known her, of course, since I was a young boy. But that particular evening, by the lake, as soon as we caught sight of each other, it was as if we were looking at each other for the first time. And I knew then that I had been wrong to go with anyone else. And I saw that I had been wicked to break one of your commandments. Rachel and I were married only a few months afterwards, and we were very happy together. Very happy indeed.

A year later, Caleb was preaching by the boats, and I went to listen to him. And I suppose you could say that he just had me fairly entranced. He was so full of life – and so confident. In fact, he was quite wonderful. So, when his preaching was over, I stayed behind to talk to him. Well, after we'd been talking together for a while, and I had listened to his voice and looked into those eyes of his, I knew that Caleb had only to say the word and I would follow him – because in some odd kind of fashion I suppose you could say I had a sort of love for him. So when Caleb asked me to be one of his disciples I said 'yes'. And I followed him everywhere he went.

And I left my wife Rachel behind. After all, what else could I do? The crowds got rough sometimes. I couldn't take a woman with me. So for a time I had to desert Rachel, and I beg her forgiveness for it. Indeed I do. And I beg your forgiveness, Lord, for all my sins.

So let me suffer, oh God. Let *me* suffer – not Caleb. Let at least *some* of his pain be shared by me. Let my body be punished for the sins it has committed.

But do not kill me, Lord. Please spare me. At least let me live through the next few days, so I can be here to see Caleb rise from the dead. Let me live to see his body smooth and straight again. Let me live to see the light shining round his head when he returns to earth to rule in his power and glory. Let me see him in the hour of his triumph. For I love your son, oh God. I love him dearly.

CHAPTER TWO

His eyes are still closed. And your devout and humble servant, Gomer, gives thanks for it. I do indeed.

Caleb is deep in the trance you sent to him in your mercy, God. Just now he almost looked as if he was dead. But I could see he was alive from the rise and fall of his chest. But please don't let him awake and go through the agonies of this morning. That was horrible. Please don't let his convulsions start again. Please hear me, God.

Caleb is the Messiah. I'm convinced of it, God. Our Master is also a wonderful person. So, I daresay, were the other prophets. But somehow I don't feel I would have liked them quite so much.

Are you listening, God? I trust so. But of course you must be listening. After all, this is an important occasion. I wouldn't be surprised if it doesn't turn out to be the most important occasion the world has ever seen – apart from the moment when you created it, of course. But what I want to know is this. How much longer has Caleb got to suffer? You must be watching, God. So you must know that his pain, when he is conscious for one instant, can seem to last for an hour. So why can't he die? Why can't he die and be buried – and come back to us all the sooner? It's when he comes back – that is the moment we're all waiting for.

Please listen to me, God, because I need your help badly. And in a way you could say that it's for my own sake I need it. I do indeed. The plain truth of the matter is that I'm very worried about the funds. As you know, I'm the treasurer. So what am I to do with them?

I didn't like to mention this to you last week – I mean, it would have been in bad taste – but what if the Master *doesn't* rise from the dead? When I hinted I was a bit worried about the money, what does the Master, your son, say to me? 'Gomer,' he says, 'you know where the money's hidden, don't you? You haven't forgotten?' That's his question. 'Well, of course I know, Master,' I answer. 'Of course I haven't forgot. But what I would like to be told,' I say to the Master, 'is what you want done with all that silver? We have quite a lot there,

116

you know. And I don't like to see money lying idle. Wouldn't it be wiser to invest it? I know a temple-merchant who's very discreet. He never asks where the money comes from – so long as it's there. In fact, before I met you, Master, in the days when I made a bit from my tax-collecting on the side, I'd always go to Emmanuel to make a private investment. 'Manny,' I'd tell him, 'here's some cash. Invest it for me.' As simple as that. 'Excellent, excellent,' my friend Manny would say. 'I'm glad you've come into another inheritance.' 'Really, he's most reliable,' I told the Master. 'So why don't you let me invest the cash with Emmanuel?'

And do you know, God, what the Master answered? Well, of course you do, if you were listening. The Master said, 'There's not time.' Just like that. 'I don't understand, Master,' I replied. 'I've got time, and Manny has got all the time in the world – especially when it's a question of a cash investment.'

Then you may well have heard what your son answered. 'There's not time,' your son said, 'because I'll be back with you all inside of a week, and then there'll be no need for any money at all.' Those were his words.

'No need for money!' I exclaimed. 'There's been a need for money ever since Eve bought the apple off that wily old serpent.' And the Master laughed. 'Oh, Gomer,' he said, 'what a surprise you are going to get when I come back to earth!' And then he gave me one of those wonderful smiles of his. But I was a bit worried. 'I hope I'm not going to get an unpleasant surprise,' I said.

Then, immediately, the smile left the Master's face and when he spoke, his voice was very gentle. 'No,' he said – so quiet I could hardly hear him, 'you won't get an unpleasant surprise, Gomer, because you've got more virtue than you think. You'll be joyfully surprised – because you'll see how much happier people will be when there's no need for money, when there's no more need to sweat and grasp and cheat and kill to get it.'

So there it is, God. And I'd better tell you where I've put the money. It's buried beneath the seventh fig tree from the left as you go into His Excellency Joseph's garden, here in Jerusalem. And even the senator himself doesn't know the fact. Leah let us into the garden last night when things were getting difficult, and I buried the money when she had gone away to talk to Ben. I hope you're listening, God. I do hope so – even though I was once a sinner and fiddled those taxes in the days when I was a collector. But I've hardly sinned at all since the Master came along. So I reckon I deserve to be listened to in my own little way.

So please God, please end the Master's suffering, and bring him back to reign in glory. But let it be soon – because I can't help worrying. I mean, you and the Master and myself are the only ones who know how much there is buried there, so I can't help being rather concerned. You see, sometimes in my mind I go into Joseph's garden again, and I begin counting. One, two, three, four fig trees – five, six – and then, God, when I look at that seventh tree, well, I simply can't help it – I can't help feeling just a little bit tempted.

So please bring the Master back soon, God. Bring him back soon.

CHAPTER THREE

And I, your young servant Merab, I admit I didn't want to come here. I admit, dear Lord, that it was Leah who forced me into it because I was afraid to come. 'Merab,' Leah said, 'but for Caleb healing my arm that morning, I don't mind telling you that you'd no longer be working for Master Joseph. You were a wicked girl, Merab,' she said. 'And I'd have had you dismissed but for Caleb. So the least you can do is to go up to the hill with me and pray for him.'

So I climbed up here with her, dear Lord, and it wasn't as bad as I feared – because he's in a kind of swoon. And I've said all my prayers. And now I've done with praying, what am I to do next? I can't go home without Leah, and she hasn't shown a sign of moving. How she can stay kneeling for such a long time I just can't imagine. And at her age, too.

But what about those three soldiers drinking? You wouldn't think they'd be allowed to swig down wine while a man's dying on the cross. I know they are here as a guard to prevent a rescue, but they're an odd lot just the same. And what about the centurion? He's a strange kind of person to have got made an officer. When he turns up at Caleb's cross on his round of the others on the hill, he does nothing to stop the guards here drinking. He just doesn't seem to notice. And why does he keep staring up at the sky? Does he expect a sign from the clouds or something? And he really looks quite nervous.

That young soldier closest to me is getting drunk. With such light-coloured skin he's probably a conscript from the north somewhere. In a way he reminds me of Ephron with that big mop of black hair and those large dark eyes. But he hasn't even given me a glance. Not once. I don't know what's wrong with him. I know I oughtn't to – but I do miss Ephron. I miss him terribly – particularly at night.

I've said my prayer for Caleb, dear Lord. So now can I have a prayer just for myself?

Oh Lord, please listen to me – even if I did steal a plate and things. Please forgive me my wickedness. I knew it was wrong to lie with a man who wasn't my husband. But Ephron did promise to marry me – and when we got into the darkness of that cave there was no stopping him. But I'll try not to sin again, dear Lord. I'll really try hard. And that's what brings me to the reason for this prayer, Lord . . . Please find me a man I can love who'll marry me lawfully. A man as handsome as Ephron, of course, and as strong. If you do, Lord, I'll work hard in Master Joseph's house, and I'll never steal again. But please let me feel once more a man's arms holding me. Let me feel him warm and throbbing. Let me kiss the skin of his shoulder. Let me feel the fierceness of him, piercing me in joy and in pain. If you'll do this, dear Lord, I will never sin again. I'll obey all the commandments, and I know them what is more. I will worship no other God – or graven image, come to that. I won't take your name in vain. I'll keep the Sabbath – I always have done, when I was given the chance. I'll honour my father and mother – I didn't know my father, and my mother's dead. But I'll honour them just the same. I won't kill. And I certainly won't commit adultery – there'll be no need to. I won't bear false witness. And I won't covet anything my neighbour's got – why should I – when I'll have what I most need in the world?

Not only will I keep your commandments. I'll do my work in Master Joseph's house cheerfully. I won't sulk or be insolent – not even with Leah. But if I'm really good, then please send me the young man that's to be my husband quickly. Please let him look just like Ephron did – with heavy shoulders and all that. But can he be kinder to me than Ephron, and not beat me about? And please can he be dutiful to all your commandments? For instance, I wouldn't want him to commit adultery.

That young soldier swigging away at his wine is handsome in a way, I do admit. And he's certainly well made. But now I come to look closer I can see that he's not a patch on Ephron.

Listen, dear Lord, listen to Merab's prayer. Look down, dear Lord, on your people. Grant us our desires, if they're proper ones. And if they're improper ones, then take the desire away from us. And please spare Caleb any more suffering. Take his spirit to join you in heaven. But let him rest there a while from all his labours – before he comes back to reign on earth – because he must be so full of pain and so very tired.

CHAPTER FOUR

Listen, oh Lord, to the prayer of Manasseh . . . Kill . . . Kill them, Lord. Kill them, oh God of Israel. On my knees I beg you – let me see the Romans beaten to the ground. Every one of them – from the Governor in his Palace to these three young louts here. Look at them – sitting there, swilling down liquor beneath the cross while a great man suffers. A great man and a true prophet.

I can't find the proper words to say what I mean. But you know me, Lord. You know that Manasseh has been honest all his life. You know he has learned the scriptures and prayed to you night and day. You know he has tried in his time to rid your Kingdom of the Roman heathens.

Well, Manasseh is getting to be an old man now, and what he truly wants with all his heart is to see your Kingdom come to Israel. He wants to see you rule over your own chosen people.

The words come hard – except when they are taken from the scriptures of the prophets that have become a part of my very thoughts. So let me say this. You, dear Lord, most high and terrible, will subdue the nations under the feet of your own people. You are the ruler of the world. You made the great lights of heaven. You slew famous Kings and gave us their land for a heritage. And then – because of our sins – you let the Romans invade our country. You allowed them to conquer us.

But now we have put up with enough, and we have repented. So give us the strength to destroy our oppressors. Punish them for their iniquity. Send the sword and pestilence among them. Curse the Romans. Let the dogs eat their rotting corpses.

And save your prophet, Caleb. Give him power of endurance. Lend him strength to survive his agony. Let him live to preach the wonders of your Kingdom. Spare him terror. Spare him in the hours of darkness. Spare him in the cold of the tomb. Cover him soon with night. Then, cover the moon, Lord. Pull clouds over the stars. Darken the sky with rain. And let an old man have one more chance to be put to the test. Let darkness come soon, Lord. Let it come soon.

CHAPTER FIVE

Open your eyes for an instant, dear Lord. Look at your faithful disciple Leah, still kneeling by your cross.

Lord, how could you bear it? How could you abide to let that wretched crowd jeer and shout at you as you climbed the hill? And now – how can you stay there suffering while those soldiers loll about drinking wine? Roman filth they are, all three of them – even if they are only conscripts. And I don't care if they do hear me saying it. Show them who you are, Lord. Free one of your hands from the nail. Free your hand and heal its scar in a flash – as you healed my arm. *That* would give them a shock.

You haven't opened your eyes for quite a while, dear Lord. And in your anguish these last two days, I don't know if you've been aware who has been here praying. But when you regain your senses, you'll see that almost all of them – almost all your disciples have gone. Two or three of them admitted they were afraid, and the other half decided they didn't believe in your teachings after all. But Gomer and Ben are still here. And so is Manasseh – but I suspect he's here at Master Joseph's ordering. Little Merab is here with me – though we'll have to go back to the house presently. We've been allowed out for a while before sunset.

Merab's a sly little harlot. Look at her breast heaving as if she were crying her heart out. Don't believe it. She's just over-excited. Why, only a short while ago, I saw her slip her hands away from her eyes and take a look at that young soldier who's been drinking even more than the other two. Quite an attractive youngster he is. Syrian I would guess – with that thick curly hair and those big eyes. Well built, too. You can't help feeling sorry for some of the conscripts in the legion. Look at the way he's pouring out the wine for himself.

Master Joseph has just been round to whisper a word to Gomer and Ben. And I couldn't help hearing what he said. He told them that Caiaphas has given an order for the disciples to be arrested, and the senate police will be bound to search the hill for them. So Joseph has advised Gomer and Ben to go back to Galilee. I can see they're not too pleased about it, but Master Joseph was quite insistent, and it looks as if they're leaving.

That young Syrian soldier is so drunk now there are tears running down his cheeks. Disgusting it is. He's handsome though – I'll say that for him. He'll make a good husband to some Syrian girl. He reminds me of Tobiah.

He'd have married me, Tobiah would, I'm almost sure of it, if it hadn't been for my arm. Each time Tobiah looked at me, I could see the thoughts in his mind. How can she cook and clean the house, he'd think to himself, with only one arm? But it's different now – thanks to you, dear Lord. And I'm not unpleasing to look at. I'm better than most, if the truth be told. So, thanks to you, dear Lord, there's no reason why one of these days I shouldn't find a decent man for a husband. I was looking at myself in the mirror this morning, and I can't see why a man of my own age – or even a bit older, perhaps – shouldn't want me as a wife.

After all, one can always hope . . . But if I find the right man, I'll wait until you come back, Master. Of course I will. I'll wait so you can attend the wedding-feast. But don't suffer so long, dear Lord. Don't suffer so long.

CHAPTER SIX

I have envied them deeply as I watched them praying, and to envy is an unusual experience for me – not because I am a rich man, nor because I am a member of the Sanhedrin but because envy has never been one of my faults. 'Come Joseph,' some friend would say to me when I was a boy, 'come and look at the pony I've been given.' And *my* father had never given me a pony, but I'd still go and look at my friend's pony, and I'd feel no twinge of envy. None at all. Yet tonight I am envious.

Oh God, how much I would like to lose myself in prayer! But this evening I cannot compose my mind in any constant line of thought. At every moment I cannot help remembering that what occurs in the next few hours will determine whether my Caleb lives or dies.

I try to think if there is any detail I may have forgotten. A slip of memory tonight could be fatal. I have got rid of Ben and Gomer. Leah and Merab will soon leave. Manasseh has the wine I have prepared and the sponge, safely wrapped in a cloak, together with the other medicaments I shall need. The fact that I should have studied medicine for so many years when I was a young man must, I am sure, have been preordained. Moreover, I feel that God must favour my intention or he would not have prevented me from selling the small house in that unfrequented lane close to the southern walls of the city. All is prepared there. And the sepulchre in the garden I have bought, close to the hill, has been made ready. I cannot believe I can have forgotten any part of the procedure that will soon be adopted.

I have averted my eyes from the other crosses on the hill. I have tried to disregard the screams and groans of men in torture. I keep forcing myself to recollect that if my action proves successful, then all the crosses in this place of degradation will eventually be swept away for ever.

I have been able to look at Caleb, for he has been quiet in his swoon. But now his eyes are beginning to open, and in them I can read the agony he is enduring. And now the words of the prayer I should make are beginning to enter my mind . . .

For years on end, oh God, I indulged my desires, and I was wholly selfish. Then, at last, I found a task, and I trained myself carefully. Recently, I have had to make several decisions. I hope they have been wise, though some of the means I have used have been distasteful to me. But when your chosen people are free, they will find peace and gladness again, and all Israel will be ready for your coming.

So this is my prayer. Lend courage and spirit to Caleb to endure his agony for another few hours more. It is growing dark already. Heavy rain clouds are moving towards the hill. Let him have the courage to bear his pain for only one more hour. Let him endure until darkness comes.

When darkness has fallen, I will be ready. I will take the risk. All responsibility will be mine. Mine. If my design fails, I shall take the whole blame.

So help me, God. Calm my nerves. Clear my brain. Let the design succeed, oh God. Let it succeed.

PART FOUR

CHAPTER ONE

I had bought the little house during the last years of my father's life.
I had needed a place where I could indulge my inclinations in security.
'Joseph, you must be careful,' my father had said to me during one of
his lucid periods. 'I have heard there are unpleasant rumours spreading
about you.' So I bought myself a hiding place. The price was small
because the house was situated at the end of a very meagre and rather
foul-smelling alley in a quarter of low repute. Inside, the rooms were
dark and slightly damp. But what did I care if the rooms were
obscure by day – when I visited the house only by night? What did I
care for the low reputation of the district – when I intended to use it
only for my secret pleasures? What did I care if in winter the rooms
were damp – when I had only to light a fire in the large chimney-
place in my bedroom to feel comfortably warm? Thus, even after
my father's death, I still kept on the discreet little house, for I had
grown fond of it. I enjoyed creeping down the winding alley; I enjoyed opening the heavy door, whose brass nails were covered with
verdigris, set in a tall, dank stone wall; I was delighted each time I
entered the moss-covered courtyard with its old well from which I
could draw up drinking water. The house was narrow, but three
storeys high. Most important of all, it was not overlooked. The
dimly-lit rooms pleased me. And I relished the memories of the
evenings I had spent in my bedroom, lying on the thick sheepskin
rugs spread in front of the fire, drinking wine and staring at my young
companion, and later sliding beneath the coverlet of the wide bed.

Only Manasseh and my agent knew of the existence of my secret
lair in those days. Then, shortly after I had first met him, I had taken
Raguel to the little house for a night, and he had been so delighted
with its privacy and warm-coloured furnishings that we had spent
several evenings there.

I had begun to dread Raguel's return from the Lebanon. I was sure he
would refuse to understand the vitally important political reason

which had inspired my action – quite apart from my affection for Caleb. I knew his jealousy would be inflamed by the events which had taken place. I also knew that I must lie to him. Leah who was still in my official residence had been instructed to inform the rest of my household that I had been summoned on business to my estate in Jericho. With her I had left a sealed letter telling Raguel where I was staying.

I had hoped to be able to arrange for Caleb to leave Jerusalem before Raguel returned from his holiday. But Caleb's recovery was slow. The anguish of the long hours on the cross had nearly killed him. The drugs I had been forced to administer had further weakened him. Without Manasseh's help it would have been impossible to nurse him in his illness. Never have I been more grateful for Manasseh's fortitude. Though he sometimes claims he is an old man, his vigour is remarkable. But for his strength we could never have carried Caleb's body to the garden sepulchre and thence to his present place of rest. But for Manasseh's powers of endurance, as he sat patiently beside Caleb's bed, night after night, when I had fallen into a sleep of exhaustion, I doubt if Caleb would have survived. Moreover, we both of us had the disadvantage that the sick man we were tending with such care had no wish to survive. I had foreseen that at the moment he regained consciousness and became aware that he had not perished on the cross, Caleb would experience a sense of deep shock. But I had not reckoned on the violence of it. Both Manasseh and I had been appalled by the intensity of his horror. Thereafter, Caleb would lie in his bed in the upper room, staring in silence out of the window that looked on to a flat roof. During the first few days we fed him by hand, and he made no resistance. But as the days passed by and he began slowly to recover, a change took place. One morning when Manasseh brought him food and lifted the ladle to Caleb's mouth, he refused to open his lips. He held his mouth tight shut. Manasseh put down the tray beside Caleb and left the room, hoping that Caleb would eat when he found himself alone. But when Manasseh returned a few hours later, the food had not been touched – nor had the cup of wine. For several days Caleb refused to eat or drink. At last Manasseh and I were obliged to use force. For a while Caleb resisted our efforts. Then, suddenly he gave in. He ate a little bread soaked in milk, and he swallowed a little wine. Presently, he sat up in bed and gazed out of the window in silence, his head motionless, and tears began to slide down his cheeks, falling slowly and unendingly as the hours passed by.

I had been so concerned with my daily efforts to keep Caleb alive that I had not noticed how horribly he had changed. But as I sat beside his bed, watching the tears descend, while Manasseh washed his sweating limbs, I observed the terrible alterations in his appearance. His body had been contorted by his frantic struggles of torment on the cross. His spine had been strained as if on a rack. His hands were scarred, and his legs were inflamed. But it was in his face that crucifixion had wrought its worst injury. His hair was streaked with white. His face looked lined and emaciated. When Caleb had recovered consciousness in the tomb and had seen Manasseh and me bending over him, he had suffered at that instant a slight convulsion, a contraction of the nerves in a spasm of piercing realization, which had left his mouth deformed. The left side of his upper lip was twisted.

As I sat gazing at him after Manasseh had dried his body and covered his nakedness, suddenly Caleb's face with its grey stubble of beard turned towards me. His blue eyes examined my face and recognized me. And at that instant he shuddered in a start of revulsion. Rapidly he swung his head away from me, so that he faced the wall.

Later that day, when I climbed up to his room, I found the door locked. I was alarmed, for I knew that Manasseh had given him his midday meal and had gone to the market. I knocked loudly.

'Who's there?' a hoarse voice cried out.

'It is Joseph,' I answered.

For a moment there was silence. I did not know what to expect, for it was the first time that Caleb had spoken.

'Unlock the door,' I ordered gently.

Once again there was silence.

'I am all right,' the hoarse voice called out. 'Please be kind to me and leave me in peace.'

I hesitated, then went back to the small living-room.

That evening Manasseh climbed the stairs with Caleb's supper. Once again the door was locked.

'Who is it?' Caleb demanded.

'Manasseh,' he replied. 'I've brought you supper.'

There was a pause. Then Manasseh heard the sound of Caleb limping across the room, and the door was opened to him.

When Manasseh came down into the living-room I could see he was perplexed and upset.

'Caleb has been talking to me,' he announced, speaking overloud, as he always did when he was embarrassed. 'And it's at least a good sign that Caleb is speaking again. But he's still strange in his mind. He says all kinds of things. He has asked me to give you a message, Master Joseph. I'm to say that he knows it's only due to you he is alive. He knows you tried to do right. He says he is grateful to you for trying to help him. But I have to tell you that he doesn't want to see you. He'd rather you didn't go into his room.'

From that day onward Caleb kept the door of his room locked; he would open it only for Manasseh. I was unpleasantly disturbed by Caleb's behaviour, but I could understand the reason for it. I had been responsible for saving Caleb's life, and he resented me in consequence. However, I was encouraged by Manasseh's reports that Caleb's health was steadily improving. Although Manasseh did the shopping, and although no one came to the house and I never went beyond the courtyard, there was still a risk. Manasseh might be recognized in the market and followed. The stone covering the entrance to the sepulchre might be rolled back by some inquisitive thief who might hope to find treasure buried with the corpse. Already two of the disciples had discovered the tomb was empty. Moreover, for the sake of a much *larger* bribe, the centurion might reveal that I had bribed him.

I had let it be known that Caleb's body had been buried in the sepulchre belonging to a relation of one of his disciples, and Manasseh assured me that this was now generally believed by the public. For the time being, at least, we were safe, but I could not help feeling uneasy. I was delighted that the day when Caleb would have regained his health sufficiently to leave Jerusalem was fast approaching.

When I heard from my agent that my convoy of camels had arrived from Alexandria on its monthly journey with a large caravan, I reached a decision. I sent word to Ben and Gomer in Galilee to come at once to Jerusalem. Two days later I summoned Manasseh and asked him to tell Caleb that I insisted on seeing him.

I waited impatiently in the small living-room. I had not lit the fire for the weather was quite warm. Even though the light was sombre, the red Persian carpets on the floor and the gilt furnishings and brightly-covered divans made the room seem pleasantly cheerful.

Presently Manasseh came into the room, closing the door after him.

'Well?' I asked. 'Did you give Caleb my message?'

'Yes, Master,' Manasseh grunted.

'What did he say?'

'He just nodded his head,' Manasseh answered. 'He doesn't talk much. But I think he will come downstairs to see you.'

'Are you sure he is strong enough for the journey to Alexandria?' I asked.

'Yes, I'm certain he is.'

'And I'm certain he *must* leave Jerusalem,' I said. 'Every day he is here there is a risk. And you must be quite weary of doing all the work of the house yourself.'

'Don't worry,' Manasseh replied.

He began to fumble in the pocket of his tunic. Suddenly he produced a small wooden cross.

'I've brought you a keepsake, Master,' he said. 'I made it from the same wood on which a true prophet has been crucified.'

He handed me the cross. I tried to control my distaste as I examined it, turning the polished wood round in my hand.

'Thank you, Manasseh,' I said. 'It's kind of you. But I want you to promise me that this will be the last cross you will ever make. Quite soon it will be dangerous to have one of these in any house.'

I put the cross away behind a stack of scrolls on my desk.

'Where is the Egyptian officer in charge of the convoy staying?' I asked.

'As usual, at the inn close to the Valley Gate,' Manasseh answered.

'I shall want to see him early tomorrow morning,' I announced.

As I spoke, there was a loud rapping at the outer door. Both Manasseh and I knew the familiar rhythm of that knock. Manasseh looked at me enquiringly. I nodded my head, and he walked down the stairs to open the door. The moment I had been dreading had come. I knew I could not tell Raguel the whole truth, because there would always be the possibility that he might reveal the true facts to the disciples in a fit of jealousy, and then my whole scheme would fail. A short while later, Raguel came into the room and closed the door behind him.

'Where is he?' Raguel demanded.

His face was bronzed from the sun and his hair was untidy. In the faint light of the room he looked young once again. But as I examined him closer, I saw that his lips were compressed in displeasure, and his faded eyes were narrowed beneath their lids.

'Are you not going to greet me after a month's absence?' I enquired.

'Where is he?' Raguel repeated.

'In the room on the top floor,' I answered.

'I suppose that after all your devoted care and attention, Caleb has recovered?' Raguel enquired sarcastically.

'In his body, yes,' I replied.

Raguel was glowering at me.

'I once said you would have made an excellent physician, Joseph,' he announced. 'I am now beginning to think you would have done better in politics – Roman politics. You calculate matters so adroitly.'

Even though I had expected it, I was annoyed by Raguel's tone of voice, but I was determined to control myself.

'You flatter me,' I said.

'The risk was that Caleb would die before you could take him down from the cross,' Raguel continued. 'How much did you have to pay Valerius Gratus?'

'Valerius Gratus? Nothing,' I answered.

'I am afraid I can no longer believe you,' Raguel told me.

'You appear to have forgotten the laws that govern our land,' I informed him. 'The Roman law is perfectly clear on the point. The law commands that the body of a person crucified should be delivered to those who claim it. The centurion in charge told me I could take down the body when Caleb was dead, and I could put the corpse in the sepulchre.'

'What sepulchre?'

'I did not wish Caleb's body to be thrown into a common grave,' I explained. 'Accordingly I bought a small garden which contained a sepulchre.'

'Conveniently placed, I daresay, between this house and the hill?' Raguel suggested.

'Most certainly,' I answered quietly.

'How much did you have to pay the centurion?' Raguel asked.

'There was no need for any payment. Caleb was dead when we took him down from the cross,' I stated.

'Is that what you have told Caleb?' Raguel demanded scornfully.

'Yes,' I answered. 'It is the truth.'

Raguel watched me in silence.

'I wonder why you, who are always so careful, Joseph, should take such a risk?' he asked. 'Are you so deeply in love with him?'

'I have never been in love with him,' I replied.

Raguel settled himself down on the divan beneath the window. During the last few years I have noticed it has become a habit of his to place himself in a room so that the light is behind him.

'Am I right in supposing you have sent a message to Alexandria for your house there to be prepared?' he enquired.

'Yes,' I replied.

'I really need not have asked.'

'I want Caleb to live in Egypt,' I said. 'I want him far away from this country. I don't want him recognized. But before he leaves for Alexandria I intend him to meet such of his disciples as may remain.'

'Why?' Raguel asked.

'I want them to see with their own eyes that Caleb has risen from the dead.'

'You may persuade some of Caleb's poor followers that he died on the cross,' Raguel stated. 'But please do not expect *me* to be taken in.'

I looked at Raguel calmly and steadily. It was essential that he should believe what I now told him.

'Caleb was dead when Manasseh and I took him down from the cross,' I said. 'His heart had stopped beating. We put a sheet round his body. We carried him into the cave. When we unwrapped the sheet, the body was cold. Caleb was obviously dead. Manasseh had brought aloes and myrrh and the usual medicaments for embalming. Suddenly, as we looked at the body, we beheld what seemed to be quite unbelievable. For an instant we saw the lids of Caleb's eyes flicker. There was no doubt about it in our minds – though at the time it seemed quite incredible. It was indeed a miracle. Caleb was still alive. I was trained as a doctor, so I knew what to do to get his heart working. Presently Caleb stirred. A short while later the blood was flowing in in his veins. Caleb was alive.'

'So that is what you will tell Caleb's disciples?' Raguel asked.

'Remember that Caleb cured Leah's arm – when all the specialists I had called in over the years had failed,' I answered. 'Caleb does truly possess a strong healing force. Is it not possible that what one might call a divine power does indeed run through him?'

'You have not answered my question,' Raguel stated.

133

'My reply is "yes",' I told Raguel. 'But I will tell the disciples only part of what occurred, for they would never understand the complexities of the miracle that happened in the tomb. They must simply believe the plain truth – the truth that Caleb has risen from the dead. And they must see him alive. In fact, I hope they will come here tomorrow afternoon. But they will not be told he is leaving for Egypt. When Caleb disappears from Palestine once and for all, they will believe that his preachings have come true. They will believe that he is with God. They will worship him in heaven. And they will follow his doctrines forever. And they will spread the word.'

Raguel was regarding me in perplexity.

'I fear I do not understand your reasoning, Joseph,' he said. 'I cannot comprehend your motives. When I left Galilee, you were hostile to Caleb's teachings. Why have you suddenly changed your opinion? Why should you care what Caleb's followers believe?'

'Why? Because as I travelled from Galilee to Jerusalem I realized that Providence had given me a great opportunity,' I replied. 'Let me explain. I now want Caleb's teachings to flourish. I want his fame to spread not only in this country but amongst the masses all over the world. I want his teachings to become a force throughout the Roman Empire.'

'But why? Why?'

'I want Caleb's followers to have faith,' I explained to Raguel. 'Faith that he was the Messiah, faith that the greatest miracle the world has ever known has taken place. Faith that a human being has arisen from the dead to prove that he *is* the Messiah. Then, in their zeal, his followers will propagate the words that Caleb taught, and a new religion will arise and prosper. And then, cannot you see the result? People all over the Empire will come to believe there is only one God who is all-powerful. And if they believe in a God who through his Son can triumph over death and promise eternal life to the poorest man on earth, and damnation to the richest, then how many people, do you suppose, will continue to believe in the power of an Emperor in Rome? As the new religion spreads? Increasingly fewer. Fewer people will believe in the might of the Emperor with each day that passes. So, gradually, respect for authority will be eroded, and in time the Roman Empire will crumble. Long before then its grasp will have been weakened, and our country will be free. For as the religion spreads, more people will think of Caleb as the Messiah who has come to save mankind. They will believe that *he* is their King – Caleb in heaven – rather than the Emperor in Rome.'

Raguel's eyes had grown wide with astonishment.

'Have you become insane during these last few weeks, Joseph?' he asked. 'Can you honestly believe that two or three of Caleb's disciples and a few of his followers could possibly spread a religion beyond the confines of Galilee?'

'Yes,' I answered. 'I do indeed believe such a thing is possible. First, consider the facts. Many people in Galilee know that Caleb cured men of their madness and healed Leah's arm. Moreover, all the fishermen round the lake trust Ben, and some of the village-folk even trust Gomer. When those two disciples return to Galilee and tell their friends they have in fact seen Caleb alive – after he died on the cross – and they swear to it before God, the news will travel from one end of the country to the other. And all Caleb's followers will preach his words. Next, consider the content of Caleb's doctrines. "The happiness of God's salvation will be shared by Jew and Gentile alike . . . Repent and you will be forgiven your sins . . . God will bless the poor and suffering, the outcasts and misfits of the world, the lame in spirit and deformed in mind, the humble and the sinners." What sayings could possibly have been devised more likely to appeal to the masses? Has there ever been a religion at once so simple and popular as Caleb's? Within less than five years, I promise you, the new religion will have spread to Rome. Within ten years the Roman Empire as we know it today will have collapsed.'

'Is that your only motive?' Raguel asked. 'Ambition? Desire for the success of your plan to destroy the Roman Empire? I must confess I am not sure. One can never tell with you, Joseph. For you work on two levels. You may seem to be scheming to change the balance of power in the world, while all the time you are dreaming about your little house, overlooking the harbour of Alexandria.'

'No, Raguel,' I said.

'But I suppose you *will* go to Alexandria to see Caleb when he is installed there?' Raguel enquired.

'I have to visit Egypt occasionally,' I replied.

'And you always travel alone to Alexandria,' Raguel said. 'Do you imagine I am ignorant of the reason?'

'When you see Caleb,' I said quietly, 'you will realize there is no need to be jealous.'

'Caleb is young,' Raguel replied. 'He will soon recover.'

Raguel rose from the divan and crossed to the window and looked out at the dim little courtyard. He was silent.

'Joseph,' he began, speaking in a deliberately casual voice, 'do you not sometimes think it may be time for me to leave you?'

'No,' I replied firmly. 'I most certainly do not. Surely we have been happy all these years together? At least I know that I myself have been happy and, in general, you have given me the impression of enjoying your existence. You must know that I am devoted to you. You must know that I hope you will stay with me until I die. So what has put the idea of leaving me into your head? Have you started some passionate love affair with a young friend in the Lebanon?'

'I wish I had,' Raguel said.

'Then why should you think of leaving?'

'Because sometimes you give me the impression that I am in the way,' Raguel answered.

'Sometimes I wonder if the world would not be a great deal simpler if we could read each other's hearts,' I said. 'For when it comes to the deepest and most important matters of our existence our means of communication are so obtuse that we might be two donkeys braying at each other in a stable. How easy and glib are our declarations in a momentary passion! How infinitely difficult are all true affirmations of compassion and of love!'

Raguel did not reply. Suddenly the latch of the door lifted. Raguel swung round as it creaked open and Caleb came into the room. Raguel gave a quiet gasp. I could understand the reason for it. This was the first time I had seen Caleb on his feet. Manasseh had given him a robe of mine made of heavy damascene silk which contrasted with his sad appearance. To Raguel he must seem almost unrecognizable. His hair was now grey, almost white. The injury to his spine caused him to stoop a little. The deformity of his lip had grown less but was still noticeable. The expression of his eyes was strangely distracted. He looked like a young boy disguised as an old man. Slowly he closed the door behind him and moved towards us. As he nodded to Raguel, the muscles of his face slid in a nervous spasm. Then he turned to me.

'Manasseh told me you wanted to see me,' Caleb said.

'I thought it was time you should leave your sick-room,' I told him.

Raguel had been staring at Caleb in dismay. Suddenly he looked away from him and moved towards the door.

'I will be in my old room, if you want me,' Raguel told me, and walked out quickly.

I drew up a comfortable chair for Caleb, and he sat down.

'Before you say anything I want to talk to you,' Caleb said to me, stammering a little in his speech. 'I must talk to you . . . because I want to leave Jerusalem . . . Every moment I am in this house, we are all in danger . . . So I must go.'

'I promise you there is no immediate danger,' I told him. 'But I agree you should leave.'

'I must go,' Caleb repeated. 'The walls of my room oppress me. And I am sick.'

'You are better,' I told him gently. 'You are far less weak.'

'I am sick in mind,' Caleb murmured.

'Your health will improve when you get away,' I replied, enthusing confidence in my voice. 'You remember I spoke to you about my house in Alexandria? Well, you are now strong enough to travel. And there is a convoy leaving for Egypt tomorrow night. I want you to leave this country for a while. You have finished the task for which you were sent. You have shown that you are the greatest of all the prophets in our history. You are the Chosen One.'

Caleb clasped his hands tightly together and stared down at them.

'There is no need to pretend to me,' he said in his hoarse voice. 'I know. I now know.'

'You arose from the dead,' I stated.

'No, Joseph,' he replied.

'You were dead. I have told you so again and again,' I said firmly. 'Your body was cold when we took you down from the cross. Your heart had stopped beating. You were dead when we unwrapped the sheet in the tomb.'

'For a long time I lost consciousness,' Caleb told me.

When he spoke he lifted his eyes in a look of entreaty, as if beseeching me to believe what he had said.

'You were dead,' I repeated. 'You were crucified. And on the cross you died. But God raised you from death.'

Caleb unclasped his hands and stretched them out so that the scars left by the nails showed on his palms.

'If God had wanted to raise me from the dead, he would have

listened when I cried out to him,' Caleb said. 'He would have raised my body without any blemish. He would have raised my spirit intact – brilliant and joyful. But look at me, Joseph. Look at me.'

I walked to the window and stared out at the dusk gathering over the courtyard. I could not bear to witness the pain in Caleb's eyes. I was now very much aware that I was in love with him.

'We know there are things beyond our understanding,' I said quietly. 'Could you understand how you cured Leah's arm? While you were in Galilee you employed simple words and images to convey your thoughts to the people who listened to you. When God spoke to you, is it not possible that he also used simple words to convey his message – because the full truth was too complicated for you to grasp? Do you not realize that your mission has already been fulfilled? You have risen from the dead. Your name will live for ever, I tell you. For ever and ever.'

'My name will be forgotten,' Caleb answered. 'Within a few years, I will be – I will be just one more fanatic who was crucified.'

I went to the side-table and poured out two cups of wine from the flask.

'You will have disciples and followers in Galilee,' I told him, handing him one of the cups. 'Those who believe in you will preach your teachings.'

'They will have lost what faith they had in me,' Caleb answered.

'When your disciples see you have risen from the dead?' I demanded. 'When they see you are alive, with the wounds still in your hands? Why – then they will believe in you with all their hearts. Even if only three or four of your followers now see you alive, they will spread the news to all the others.'

Caleb drank from his cup.

'If they saw me now, then perhaps,' Caleb replied, 'perhaps they might believe. But they will not see me.'

'Why not?' I asked. 'We know we can trust them.'

I sat down in the chair facing Caleb. I spoke very gently.

'Caleb,' I began, 'I have taken a decision. I honestly think that when you have had time to consider it you will approve of what I have done. I have sent word to Gomer and Ben. They are travelling back to Jerusalem. Arrangements have been made for them to stay secretly in the city. I have asked them to come here tomorrow.'

'To see me?' Caleb asked.

'Yes, Caleb,' I answered.

'No!' Caleb cried out hoarsely. 'I will not meet them. I cannot.'

'Cannot?' I enquired. 'Why?'

'I could not bear to look in their eyes – when they learn the truth,' Caleb stammered.

'What truth?' I asked.

Caleb took a long drink of wine.

'That I am a plain man,' he answered. 'A man who has been made hideously aware of the flesh. A man who is still encompassed by his body.'

'Listen, Caleb,' I said. 'I have told you that I know you died on the cross and arose from the dead. But even if you do not believe me, surely you must want your teachings to survive? Surely you must want mankind to reap the benefit of the truth which you have preached and of the inspiration for which you have suffered? Do you wish to deny to the people the blessing of all that you have taught?'

Caleb was looking at me, but I was almost certain that he could not see me. His mind, for a while at least, had forgotten my presence. When I had first installed him in the upper room I would often hear him talking to himself as I climbed the stairs. He was once again in one of the trance-like moods I had known when he had visited my house in Galilee.

'I had gifts,' he said. 'Sometimes – I could work miracles. I may have been a prophet. God – some God must have been working through me . . . Perhaps the last miracle is that I am alive. But I thought – on the cross, I thought I would be rid of my flesh. I would leave my body, with its pain and sweat and excrement. I believed – I believed I would rise into the air, clean as an arrow, to reach – to reach God. But I was wrong. Very wrong. Foolish.'

'No, Caleb,' I said quietly.

But he was no longer listening. In silence he drank the wine and put down the cup on the table beside him.

'Foolish,' he repeated. 'Presumptuous and wickedly vain. Impiously vain.'

Caleb stopped speaking. His soft eyes watched me without expression. His mind once again had been occluded.

CHAPTER TWO

'Vain,' I repeated to Joseph, 'vain.' And then the darkness seemed to fall down on me like a cloak, and I could reason no more ...

It is very cold where I dwell most of these days. It is cold and dark in the corridor of my mind. And I drank Joseph's wine in the hope that it would warm a part of the black tomb in which, from time to time, I am still imprisoned.

But there is a door to the sepulchre, and I must never pass through that door, for then I would suffer all my agonies all over again. I thought I had bolted the door. I had locked it. But now it is ajar, and through its opening I can see back into the past.

Since the days I was a child, I tried – I tried not to let anyone touch me – neither man nor woman, nor girl nor boy. As I had told Joseph, I was afraid of being touched ... I was afraid of it.

That morning in the court of the temple, when the police with their staves came to arrest me, they grabbed hold of me. And my disgust was so strong that I retched. I could feel their hands burning my wrists, burning my shoulders. I could not control my revulsion. I struggled. In my frenzy I struck out at one of them. Then the soldiers closed in on me. I was alone. My disciples had fled, for they had no weapons, and they were outnumbered. What else could they do? So there were no witnesses. They took me into the castle and threw me into a prison cell. There they held me fast, while the man I had hit began striking me – all over my face and my body. 'Don't mark him too much,' the centurion shouted out. 'Don't forget we may have to take him before their rotten High Priest.'

But the High Priest was at a meeting of the Sanhedrin. And from the meeting he hurried to a dinner party. When they took me to his house, he was in bed and asleep. So I was brought back to the barracks and put into my cell. I heard the centurion detail a soldier on duty to watch me in case I tried to kill myself in the night. He was a soldier I had not seen before. He was a young Syrian conscript of about my own age. But he was taller and more strongly built. He sat there in the cell, looking at me as I lay on the floor. Then he smiled and said, 'Mehdi's given you a proper beating, hasn't he?' The young soldier spoke with the sing-song accent the Syrians have. 'You won't sleep with those scars and bruises all over you,' he said. 'I'll go and fetch some oil to soothe them.' He walked out, locking the cell-door after him. And I was grateful. The young conscript had a pleasing look about him, with his light-coloured skin and thick curly hair and dark eyes.

Presently he came back with a jar of oil. He locked the door behind him. 'Take off your robe,' he said, 'and I'll rub you down.' I felt numbed with weariness. I was too tired and confused to explain that I could not bear to be touched. The young soldier took my robe, folded it, and spread it out on the floor. He gestured to me to lie down on it. Then he turned away and blew out the lamp, so the cell was in darkness. 'There are cracks in the door,' he whispered. 'I wouldn't want anyone to see me looking after you.' Then he knelt down beside me. A faint light filtered into the cell from the lamp-lit corridor outside. The soldier began rubbing the oil into my skin. His hands were rough, but he was very gentle. I was not afraid. I was surprised to discover that I did not mind his hands sliding over me. Soon my pains grew less, and my aching limbs were calmed.

As the soldier's hands moved over my body, stroking my chest and thighs, I began to feel soothed. I could feel warmth beginning to creep over me. And still the gentle hands moved in their rhythm. Then, suddenly, it began . . . Suddenly, warmth seemed to glow across my body, spreading all over me, invading my veins, causing my blood to surge and the temples of my head to throb. And I became aware – became alive in all my being. I felt my heart beating. There was a wild murmuring in my ears. I could feel the life in me swelling in a slow wave of excitement.

Soon the hands of the young soldier stopped moving. In the darkness, I heard a rustle as he unfastened his tunic. I heard a faint clink as his belt dropped on to the floor. I knew the reason for this – though I tried to conceal it from myself. For an instant there was silence. I knew that if I turned my eyes and beheld him I would lose the last traces of control over myself. But it was as if I no longer had any power over my eyes: I had lost dominion over them. I could no more control them than I could my quivering limbs. So I turned my head, and I looked up at the soldier. He was standing, gazing down at me, with his large, dark eyes. His tawny body was smooth and hard as marble. Yet I could feel the warmth of him, and I could see his limbs, taut and trembling. I could see the force of his inflamed passion.

Then he lowered himself slowly to the ground and lay beside me, and his arms seized hold of me. But I was not afraid. For a moment he was motionless. Then he began to move, his muscles striving brutally in their passion. But I was still not afraid, and I let him do as he wanted. He forced himself against me as if he would kill me. Then, I could feel the pain swelling inside me. His hands were now clutching at me in a frenzy. I felt his force stir within me. Then came waves of shame – waves of shame, sweeping over me – and then a surge of ecstasy that reached beyond all anguish.

The next day, when they began to whip me, when I felt the thongs of the scourge biting into my flesh, I was glad – because each stab of pain made me remember I was still alive. My whole being seemed to throb with each lash. I could feel the surge of my blood, and I exulted, because at last I knew that my spirit was not separated from me. It existed in a body made of muscle and flesh.

Even after they had fixed me on to the cross, I was not afraid. Joseph had told me that a man could live for several days on that terrible device of agony. But when I felt the blood pouring from my hands, I was certain I would die. And then, all my suffering would be at an end. And with my resurrection, the Kingdom of God would come on earth. And then all suffering throughout the world would be assuaged and all tears wiped away.

But after a while the bleeding stopped, and soon the real agony began. Soon it became unbearable. Frantically, I tried to tear my hands away from the nails. I tried to free my feet from the cords that bound them. But each effort I made brought on a stab of anguish so intense I was sure I must faint. Yet I did not lose consciousness. And I decided I must try to suffer patiently the torment that the prophets had foretold I must endure before God came to save me.

To distract my mind – I tried to make myself think of the vineyard in which I had worked when I was a child. It was surrounded partly by a fence – I forced myself to recollect – and partly by a hedgerow of prickly shrubs. The young vines were planted in straight rows, lying apart a few spans more than a man's height. Desperately I forced myself to remember each precise detail. The vines were pruned each spring. There was a high watch-tower on a hill overlooking the vineyard where my father or some member of his family could keep guard when the grapes were ripening. This structure, I remembered, had a roof to protect the watcher from the heat of the sun.

As my pains grew more fierce, I found it harder to fix my mind on that lovely vineyard on the slopes above Cana. When the grapes were mature, they were gathered into baskets and taken to the great wine-press which was hewn out of the rock. The treading of the wine by all the labourers, shouting and singing together, was one of the happiest occasions of the year. We stored the fermenting wine in new goatskin bags. And when the harvest of grapes had been gathered, we would allow all the poor of the village to come into our vineyard to pick any bunches that remained. As I thought about our vineyard, it was as if I were thinking of some place so far away that it lay at the very extremity of the earth. Then, abruptly, the vineyard vanished – because in my head and chest were now beginning pains so terrible I could not stop myself from crying out in my torture.

Presently I made myself repeat the words of the scriptures I had learned from the Essenes. 'Even though I lie in the valley of death, God will not leave me. He will rescue me and revive me. He will never allow my soul to perish in the grave. His presence will never leave me.' And slowly dawn came. But I still remained conscious. I now began to pray to God to deliver me. I besought him to let me die. 'I have suffered enough,' I told him. 'I can bear no more.' But my anguish still continued, and I never lost consciousness – not even in the heat of noon.

Then, with every particle of strength I could summon, I tried to wrench my spirit away from my body – away from the body which had deceived me so recently by pretending it could offer me an ecstasy of joy – when all that this flesh was made for, I now realized, was to pull my soul down into hell. I hated my body because I knew that its bones and sinews could destroy my spirit forever.

When the sun began to set that evening, I knew I was alone. I knew, finally, that God had forsaken me. At that moment I was certain I would never rise from the cross. I was alone – imprisoned in my body. And my body was being tortured. My body had become the master of my spirit. My body was burning with thirst.

As it grew darker and the stars came out into the night, they no longer affirmed to me the wonders of God. They pierced the darkness in a glittering mockery of mankind struggling like so many ants below them in endless toil and endless misery. It was then that I cried out aloud again, and it was then that Manasseh fixed a sponge soaked in wine on to the end of a stick and put it to my lips, and I sucked at it greedily, time and again.

For the first time I became dimly aware of some of the friends I had made in the days before my spirit was broken. They were kneeling at a distance from the cross. And, at my feet, were three Roman soldiers with empty wine-flasks around them. Two of them were asleep, but the third soldier was awake, and he was crying. Suddenly, I recognized the Syrian conscript who had been with me in the cell. Perhaps he was crying at the sight of the body he had taken in his arms being now stretched out and distorted on a rack. If only he could understand that what happened to my body no longer had any consequence.

There was no God, I was now convinced. My preaching had been in vain. My life had been an illusion. When the moon arose its cold light peered down indifferently at a little man – one of the many millions of people suffering in the world – a little man, nailed to a little cross.

Gradually I could feel that my limbs were becoming rigid. Soon I seemed to feel that my heart was growing numb. The pain in my head was now dull. Then, I knew at last I was going to die, and I was glad. I wanted to die – because if there was a God he must indeed have abandoned me. I no longer believed I would rise from the dead. All I now prayed for was extinction – the end of pain, the end of suffering, the end of all effort. My only desire in the world was for oblivion.

And at last oblivion came.

But then – perhaps it was only a few hours later, though it seemed like many hundreds of years – then, through a void of darkness, imperceptibly and vaguely, as if in a dream, I began to grow aware ... Awareness came ... Awareness I was still alive ...

CHAPTER THREE

'After the torture,' Caleb told me, 'after the wine on the sponge, there came oblivion. But after some long time, slowly, slowly, I awoke from my oblivion, and I realized that what I had experienced on the cross had not been a terrible dream. It had been real, Joseph. It had been true . . . Awareness came back to me – after what seemed many hundreds of years. Awareness that I was still alive.'

'It seemed many years – because you were dead,' I told Caleb. 'You arose from death.'

'I was alive,' Caleb repeated. 'And as I felt the blood flowing back into my body, so could I feel the the despair flowing back into my heart. For I remembered I was still alone – because God had left me.'

'You were alive because God saved you,' I told Caleb.

'Is that what you believe, Joseph?' he asked.

'God was with you,' I said. 'That you are here in this room proves it.'

'It proves I survived two days of torture,' Caleb replied.

'You were dead, I tell you. Life was extinct in you,' I said. 'I am not lying, Caleb. You have risen from the dead. Your disciples have only to see you to believe it. They will believe because it is the truth.'

'If my followers believed I was the Messiah and had risen from the dead,' Caleb said, speaking very slowly, 'and if the Messiah did not return to earth with God and all his angels to judge mankind, then what would my followers think? They would think that the priests, Pharisees, Sadducees, members of the Sanhedrin and Romans were guilty for bringing about my crucifixion . . . Presently, they would begin to feel guilty in their own hearts because they themselves had been unable to prevent it. And then? Then people would say that it was the evil inherent in mankind which caused my suffering and crucifixion.'

Caleb rose and walked across to the table and stood, staring for a while in silence out of the window in the darkening courtyard.

'And for its crime, mankind would forever be held guilty,' he cried hoarsely. 'Guilty for the scourging, guilty for the long hours of torture, guilty for the murder on the cross. Guilt would be the weapon priests would use to subdue the hearts of men.'

Caleb picked up the wooden cross that Manasseh had made me and which I had put down on the table. He held up the cross and looked at it in the waning light.

'This would be the symbol of their guilt,' he said, 'the emblem of their religion. The cross – the effigy of death, the token of misery . . . The cross – rather than a sign which could remind mankind that the purpose of life is in living and in creation. The cross – rather than a spray of water or a blade of wheat. The cross – rather than a flower or an image of the sun.'

'No, Caleb, you are wrong,' I said. 'Your reasoning is confused. People will indeed revere the cross, but only because it will be a symbol of the triumph of the spirit over death. Above all, you must remember that if any of your disciples see you alive, then they and your followers will believe in your teachings. They will believe the sick will be comforted. They will believe the humble will inherit the earth. You have given them hope. But they have seen you die on the cross. If they now see you alive, their hope will be confirmed. And through them, you will have given hope to all mankind – to all mankind until the end of the world.'

Caleb was silent. The door opened, and Manasseh came in.

'The officer of the convoy is here, Master,' he announced.

'Thank you, Manasseh,' I replied. 'Tell him I will join him immediately.'

For an instant Manasseh glanced at the wooden cross in Caleb's hand. Then he nodded his head and left the room. I turned to Caleb. He was now staring fixedly at the cross.

'Remember what I have told you, Caleb,' I said. 'The decision is for you to make.'

CHAPTER FOUR

I stood in the room I had sometimes occupied in the days soon after I had met Joseph and became his companion. I gazed out of the window at the fading light in the little courtyard.

Joseph must probably think I had left the living-room hurriedly when Caleb came in because I had been shocked by his appearance. But he would be wrong. I had indeed been distressed by the sight of Caleb. Obviously he had suffered most terribly. But he was young, and time would help him to recover. Caleb had not disturbed me unduly. I had been more upset by Joseph's own manner – ever since the moment I had entered the room. During the weeks I had been away in the Lebanon, Joseph had changed. There was now an odd and strained intensity about him. The hectic expression in his eyes had become far more noticeable. He had been so taut that it was as if he were exerting a constant effort of will-power to force me to believe every word he said. He was very perturbed. And his distress immediately removed the rage I had felt when I had discovered that he had tried yet again to deceive me. Then, poor Caleb came into the room. And Caleb, with his ravaged face and contorted body, clad in Joseph's old robe of white damascene silk, had reminded me of some wounded animal. Suddenly, in a flash I had become aware of the reason for Joseph's present condition. I knew the story of Simon and the dove, and of Simon's crucifixion. I knew that Joseph was still haunted by that horrid event in his life. And as I now watched him gazing at Caleb, I realized what had probably occurred in his strange mind. Caleb, with his broken body, had somehow become associated with Simon and the dove which Joseph had once found by the stream.

I stared out of the window. Dusk was falling in the courtyard. I wished I could believe in God so that I could pray for Joseph. I would pray that God would soothe the anxious cravings of his heart and bring him peace. And I would pray to God for myself . . . Let me become richer in my heart, I would pray. Let me find the spirit which will drive the jealousy from my soul and deepen my shallow mind. Release the heavy fetters around my brain. Let my spirit, untrammelled by the desires of my flesh, soar into heights of inspiration. Let the spirit of love flow into my soul so that I become the poet of my race. Let me forget what is over: Let the unsightly scrawls on my past be wiped clean from the slate. And, lastly, let Joseph be tormented no longer. Help me to set him free from his terrible obsession.

As I stood by the window, I heard a knock at the outer door. Manasseh crossed the courtyard and lifted the cover of the grille and peered through it. Then, without hesitation, he drew back the heavy bolts, so he must have known the visitor standing outside. An instant later the Egyptian officer in charge of the convoy entered the courtyard. Evidently he had come to talk with Joseph. I must take the opportunity his arrival gave me of seeing Caleb alone. I must move quickly. For I was sure that Joseph would certainly use the arrival of the caravan as an excuse to keep me safely out of the way.

Taking an oil-lamp with me, I walked softly along the passage to the living-room. As I came in, Caleb was standing by the side-table in the half darkness. He was pouring wine into his cup. He looked at me in silence with his haunted face.

'The officer in charge of the convoy has arrived,' I told him. 'He is downstairs talking with Joseph.'

'I heard someone arrive,' Caleb said. He began to drink the wine.

'Will you leave with the caravan tomorrow night?' I asked him.

Caleb did not reply. I doubt if he had heard my question. He was staring at me as if he were uncertain of what he should say.

'Raguel, do you believe I rose from the dead?' Caleb asked suddenly.

I knew that my only hope was to be ruthless with him.

'No,' I answered.

Caleb took a gulp from his cup.

'Did you *ever* believe in me?' he asked.

'I thought you could see into a person's mind,' I said.

'No longer,' Caleb answered.

'I pretended to have faith in you,' I told him, 'because I wanted you to believe you were the Messiah, so you would leave Galilee and go to Jerusalem, and be put out of our way.'

'I can understand,' Caleb murmured.

I poured myself out a cup of wine.

'But why did Joseph take such a risk to rescue you from the cross?' I demanded. 'Have you asked yourself that question?'

'I have wondered,' Caleb replied.

'Joseph's father went mad some while before he died,' I said. 'Joseph is not insane, as his father was. But sometimes he is almost deranged. You must, by now, have begun to perceive the truth. Joseph has only one ambition – success. He sees himself as leading this country in revolt. He thinks your "resurrection" can help him – because if your religion spreads across the Empire, it could undermine the power of Rome.'

As I drank, I watched Caleb carefully.

'Has Joseph told you that you died on the cross?' I asked.

Caleb was silent. I took another sip of wine.

'Yes, of course he has,' I said, answering my own question.

'How much can you remember? Do you remember Manasseh handing you a sponge of wine on a stick? Yes? Well, some time after that moment your head drooped forward, I am told, and you lost consciousness. And I will tell you *why*, Caleb. You lost consciousness because the wine in the sponge was drugged.'

Caleb's gaze was fixed on me.

'How do you know?' he asked. 'How can you be sure?'

'I was suspicious from the first,' I explained to him. 'At a crucifixion on the hill, there is always a group of women who come with wine to alleviate the victim's suffering. But I heard from Leah that Joseph sent the women away. He himself had brought wine for you, he said. Then, shortly before dusk, he dismissed Leah and Merab. He had already found an excuse to get rid of Gomer and Ben. Two hours after sunset a Roman centurion appeared and pronounced you dead. The three soldiers on guard were dismissed. Joseph and Manasseh took you down from the cross and carried you to a sepulchre in a garden close by. And in the tomb they revived you. Shortly before dawn they carried you to this house.'

'Why do you tell me this?' Caleb asked.

'Because I want you to realize that Joseph is making use of you for an insane and fraudulent reason,' I answered.

'How can I be sure you are not lying again?' Caleb asked. 'Because you were jealous, you wanted to get rid of me when I was in Galilee. You are still jealous.'

I shook my head. 'No, Caleb,' I said gently. 'I am no longer jealous.

But may I ask you an important question? Joseph has sent a message to Ben and Gomer. They are coming here secretly tomorrow evening. Will you see them?'

For an instant Caleb's face trembled.

'I have not yet decided,' he answered.

From downstairs I heard the hall door open. I glanced out into the courtyard. The Egyptian officer was leaving. I had only another minute left.

'You are sick, Caleb,' I told him. 'But you have not lost your power to reason – not by any means. You still possess your intellect.'

I paused. I concentrated my gaze on him. Then I spoke very slowly and deliberately.

'You are still responsible for your actions,' I said. 'Therefore I do not suppose that, on reflection, you will wish to be the founder of a religion that is based, if only in part, on an utter deceit.'

Swiftly I left the room.

CHAPTER FIVE

I knocked at the door. After what we had been through, I could hardly believe it possible that I would soon hear his voice again.

'Who is it?' I heard someone ask.

But something wasn't right. The strained hoarse voice didn't seem to belong to Caleb.

'Master,' I called out. 'Master, are you there? It's Gomer. I've come to see you. Please can I see you, Master?'

There was a long silence. And I began to think I might have done wrong. And I suppose it may have been presumptuous of me. But I wanted to be the first: I wanted to see him before Ben and Leah. Besides, there was a reason why I had to see him alone. So I excused myself from the room where we were gathered together with Joseph after the journey, and I crept upstairs. Manasseh had said Caleb was in the upper room. But why didn't he answer me?

Then I heard a bolt in the door being pulled back; then the key turned in the lock. I pushed open the door and walked into the room. Standing, staring at me, was a stranger dressed in a robe of white silk.

I gaped at him in confusion. Suddenly I recognized his face. It was Caleb – though he had changed terribly. I joined my hands together and raised them in salutation. His appearance was so altered I couldn't help being distraught.

'Master, forgive me,' I said. 'At first, I didn't recognize you. Master, you are alive like Joseph told us.'

Suddenly I realized I was still on my feet, so I knelt down.

'I had to see you first,' I told him hurriedly. 'I had to, so I made an excuse to leave them. Master, forgive me. And please remember that I *did* believe in you. I was there when you were on the cross. I didn't run away like some others I could name. I was there, I promise you.'

Slowly Caleb nodded his head.

'I know it, Gomer,' he said gently.

'I keep forgetting that you know, Master,' I said. 'You almost know it all. So you know what has happened.'

'Please don't kneel, Gomer,' he said, and he gestured towards a chair.

Well, I was worried about sitting down in his presence, but I was tired after the journey, and perhaps, after all, what I had to say wouldn't sound quite right if I were kneeling. So I sat down in the chair he pointed to. And he sat down opposite me.

'It was just that it didn't turn out like you said it would,' I explained. 'That was how the trouble all started. I mean, when we heard the tomb had been found empty we were amazed. But of course we waited for the third day for you to appear again. You did say the third day, Master. Well, the third day came, and the fourth and the fifth. And still you hadn't appeared. There wasn't even a sign. And after a week had gone by, well, I couldn't help being disturbed. I mean, we'd thought that on the third day you'd come back to earth to rule in glory. But another whole week passed by. And yet another, and another. And still no sign. And then it was – three days ago to be precise – then it was, that I began thinking about that silver in His Excellency Joseph's garden. And three days ago, the very day before I got the message to come here, I just happened to be in Jerusalem. And after dark – well, I went to the garden. And the very next day the wonderful news came . . . And I had tried so hard.'

Then, like the silly person I am, well, I just couldn't help it. As I looked at his face, all strange and sorrowful, something came over me, and I broke down and began to cry.

'Ever since I became a disciple, I tried with all my might,' I told him. 'I didn't keep back a single piece of the silver from the funds for myself. And then, like a fool – like a wicked fool – I went and dug it up. I took it. Every piece of it. And as you must know, Master, I took it to Manny – the very day before I got the message to come here to this house. Only one day before I was to witness the most joyous proof the world has ever been given – the final proof that God's love and goodness will prevail forever.'

Until then, I had seldom dared to look into his eyes. But now I wiped my tears and looked at him. And from the expression of his face I felt he had understood what I was trying to say.

'Dear Master, please forgive,' I said. 'Dear God, forgive. I can get the money back. I mean, it's all safely invested – though I know that's no excuse. Master, please can I be forgiven?'

Then, as I looked up at him, I saw to my astonishment that there were tears in his eyes.

'I forgive you, Gomer,' he said – and his voice sounded even more strange than before. 'I forgive you with all my heart. Dear Gomer don't cry. Please do not cry. There is nothing to cry about.'

And I could hardly believe my own ears – because he wasn't at all angry. So I couldn't understand the reason for his tears.

'Forgiven?' I asked. 'Am I forgiven? Truly forgiven?'

'Yes, Gomer,' he answered.

'Oh, my Lord and Master,' I cried. 'God in heaven be praised. God be thanked.'

So now I have been forgiven . . . And I was the very first person from Galilee – the very first of us all to see him.

CHAPTER SIX

As he walked round the room pouring out wine into our glasses, Manasseh stopped in front of me.

'You look tired, Master Joseph,' he blurted out. 'You should go and rest a while.'

'Thank you, Manasseh,' I answered. 'I am not tired – even though I may look it.'

Grumbling a little, Manasseh left us and went downstairs. In fact, I did feel unwell. But how could I rest when all was now prepared for the confrontation?

Raguel was busy with the arrangements for loading the caravan for the journey by convoy to Alexandria: he would not trouble us. Leah and Gomer had already arrived. Ben was the last to reach the house. I had waited for him because I believed his presence would provide the added influence it might require to induce Caleb to leave his room. I was now almost certain that I had at last managed to persuade Caleb he had risen from the dead. As soon as Caleb appeared events would move according to plan. I had already given instructions to the three of them to announce on their return to Galilee that they had seen Caleb on the road beyond Jericho; I had invented excuses why Gomer and Ben should have come to Jerusalem.

When Gomer left the living-room soon after he had arrived I suspected he might have gone to see Caleb. As soon as I had greeted Ben and offered him wine, I climbed up the stairs to find out what had happened. As I approached the door, I heard Gomer's voice. 'Oh my Lord and Master,' he was crying. 'God in heaven be praised.'

I needed to hear no more. The door was not locked, and I opened it. An oil-lamp was burning on the table. Caleb was sitting with his back to me. Gomer was facing him, his greasy cheeks wet with tears.

'Caleb,' I said quietly, 'your disciple Ben has arrived. He and my servant Leah whose arm you healed are waiting downstairs to see you.'

Slowly Caleb turned his face towards me. For a moment he stared at me as if he had never seen me before. Then he nodded. In silence I left the room.

'He will come,' I told Ben and Leah. 'But you must not stay for long.'

'To see him will be reward enough,' Leah said.

'To see him – and hear him talk once more,' Ben added. 'Even if we only stay a while, we shall still have beheld a miracle.'

As Ben spoke, Caleb entered and moved towards us, followed by Gomer. By the light of the lamps he looked haggard and deformed. I could see that Leah had not recognized him, for she gaped in astonishment. Ben was the first to greet him.

'Master,' Ben called out.

Then Leah looked at Caleb closer and gave a little gasp.

'Lord God, you have raised him from the dead,' she muttered.

'It is you, Master,' Ben said, stammering in his excitement. 'It is you, and you are alive.'

'Now let them try to jeer,' Leah cried in triumph. 'Now let the Roman filth try and swagger over you.'

Ben was examining him in awe. 'The scars are still raw on your hands, Master,' Ben whispered.

'Now forever will people believe in God's power and mercy,' Leah proclaimed.

Caleb stood in silence watching them. His face was drawn, and the left side of his upper lip quivered.

'You are pale, Master,' Ben said. 'But you're with us again. You are with us.'

'He is with us,' Gomer bleated suddenly. 'I had sinned . . . But I have been forgiven.'

'Now will God be praised to the ends of the earth,' Leah sang out.

'You have risen from the dead,' Ben said softly. 'But you are not a spirit. You are breathing. There's sweat on your forehead. You are still in pain, Master.'

Caleb said nothing. I forced myself to remain calm and motionless as I watched him. The moment for which I had planned with such anxiety had now come.

'He is alive,' Leah said. 'That is what counts.'

'He has risen from the tomb,' Gomer announced. 'He has proved that he is the Messiah.'

Slowly Leah knelt down before Caleb. Then, for the first time, he spoke.

'Do not kneel,' Caleb said in a faltering voice. 'Please do not kneel.'

But Leah did not seem to hear him. She was in a rapture of exaltation.

'The day cannot now be far off when God will come to reign in glory,' Leah cried out in her voice of reverence.

'Please,' Caleb repeated, 'do not kneel.'

I took Leah's hand and raised her to her feet.

'There is no need to kneel,' I said quickly. 'You must not stay long. I had asked you to witness that Caleb is alive. For he has risen from the dead. You see him now in this room. You see the proof. Let it be known. Tell the other disciples, as we agreed, that Caleb appeared to you on the road beyond Jericho. You have now seen him. Caleb is risen. Let everyone be told – all over Galilee. And from Galilee the news will spread.'

For an instant I glanced towards Caleb. His face was very white. I turned back to Ben and Gomer.

'I will help you and the other disciples as best I can,' I told them. 'But you must go now. If you are asked why you came to Jerusalem, you will remember the excuses I have given you.' I raised my hand in a gesture of dismissal. 'So you can now leave in thankfulness to God and in gladness of spirit,' I concluded.

Ben nodded in assent. Then, shyly, he turned to Caleb.

'Master,' he said, 'please speak to us before we leave. Give us your blessing.'

'Please Lord,' Leah besought him. 'Let us hear your voice once more.'

Caleb looked at them in silence. Then he glanced towards the door, and for a moment I thought he would leave. But he raised his head and looked towards them steadily.

'I am here and alive,' Caleb said, speaking very softly. 'But I have changed. I have been changed by suffering. I believe – I believe, in some way, I died on the cross. I believe in some way I came to life again.'

'Indeed, Master Joseph has told us how you rose from the dead,' Leah said. 'For it was all written by the prophets – how the Son of God must suffer and be crucified and rise again.'

'Surely he is the Redeemer,' Gomer announced.

There was silence. They were all looking towards Caleb. I would have spoken, but I feared to use words that might influence Caleb against me and destroy my plan.

'Master, you are silent,' Ben said.

Caleb stared at him; his stricken face was aghast, his lip was quivering.

'Master, forgive me,' Ben continued in his shy, diffident way. 'But there is one question – one question I need to ask. Have I your leave to ask it?'

'Yes, Ben,' Caleb answered after a pause. 'Of course you may ask it.'

The very moment I had dreaded for so many days had come. And there was nothing more that I could do to influence the outcome of it.

In a kind of fascinated terror I watched Ben's broad hands writhing nervously together.

'Are you?' Ben stammered, then stopped in embarrassment. There was silence. An instant later he managed to speak again. 'Are you the Messiah?' he blurted out.

'What more proof do you want?' Leah demanded.

'Are you,' Ben repeated, 'are you the Son of God?'

Caleb looked at Ben desperately.

'I have always told you, Ben,' Caleb said. 'We are all the children of God.'

Ben clasped his hands together. His face held the anxious yet determined expression of a swimmer who is about to attempt a dangerous plunge.

'Are you the Messiah?' Ben asked resolutely.

'How can you be so senseless?' Leah demanded indignantly.

'He has told us, Ben,' Gomer murmured.

'Are you?' Ben repeated.

An oil-lamp was burning on a table close to Caleb, and he lowered his eyes, and began staring at it intently.

'Since I came back to consciousness,' Caleb said, speaking slowly and hesitantly, 'since my eyes opened in the darkness of the tomb, I have had no communication with God. No voice . . . No words . . . No sign . . . Therefore I can be certain of nothing . . . I may be alive because God in his mercy raised me from the dead.'

Caleb lifted his head and glanced for an instant towards me. And immediately I was afraid.

'But I may be alive merely because I lost consciousness and fell into a trance,' Caleb continued, speaking in a measured and deliberate tone. 'I may have fallen into this trance because the wine in the sponge that Manasseh handed up to me was drugged.'

'Drugged?' Ben asked in astonishment.

'Who could have drugged it?' Leah cried.

Caleb turned his head and looked straight into my eyes.

'It was drugged by you, Joseph,' he said.

'No,' I answered quietly.

Caleb's gaze was still fixed on me.

'Then can I send for Manasseh?' Caleb asked. 'Can I put the same question to him?'

'Yes,' I replied, without hesitation.

'Ben,' Caleb said, 'will you please go and ask Manasseh to come here?'

Ben nodded and went out. I was now certain that Raguel must somehow have discovered about my use of drugs. I remembered that while I had been talking to the convoy officer the previous day Raguel must have certainly had time for a brief word with Caleb. However, I was not unduly alarmed. I turned to Caleb.

'Those who have been disappointed by life can always blame external circumstances,' I told him, by way of explanation. 'Those who are disappointed by their own selves are the ones who become envious and jealous. And their jealousy makes them want to destroy.'

'That may be so,' Caleb replied.

'Excuse me, Excellency,' Gomer said, tugging nervously at his robes, 'but will Manasseh know about the wine?'

'If the wine had been drugged? Of course Manasseh would have known,' I answered firmly.

Leah turned on Gomer with a sudden violence.

'How can you believe that Master Joseph would lie to us?' she demanded indignantly. 'If he says the wine wasn't drugged, then that is an end to it.'

'Sometimes a man tells a lie from a sense of duty,' Caleb said quietly. 'Or he lies from fear, or from ambition. Is that not so, Joseph?'

'Sometimes truth runs along alleys so dark that all men's eyes cannot follow it,' I answered. 'Sometimes truth must serve a larger purpose. It must bend for the sake of a cause or a religion.'

Ben came back into the room with Manasseh. I watched them calmly. I was sure that Manasseh would not betray my secret. I avoided looking at him. Manasseh moved towards Caleb.

'You sent for me?' he asked.

'Yes, Manasseh,' Caleb replied. 'These last weeks while you have looked after me so well, we have never spoken of the night I was taken down from the cross, because neither of us wanted to. But now I have a question to ask you, Manasseh. And I think I shall know if you answer it truthfully, or if from loyalty or kindness you tell me a lie. Soon after sunset that last evening on the hill, you handed up to me a sponge soaked in wine.'

'I did,' Manasseh said.

'Was the wine drugged?' Caleb asked.

'No,' Manasseh replied. 'Never.'

'But how could you tell if the wine was drugged?' Ben asked Manasseh.

'Because I poured it myself from the vat into the wineskin,' Manasseh answered. 'Because I had a drink from it myself on the hill.'

'No,' Gomer blurted out suddenly, and then put his hand to his mouth in confusion.

They now spoke so fast – their words sometimes overlapping each other's – that it was impossible for me to interrupt.

'Do you call me a liar?' Manasseh demanded loudly.

'No,' Gomer replied, blushing in embarrassment. 'I mean, I would never dream of thinking such a thing. I'm only saying that you must have inadvertently made a mistake. Because I saw you drinking, Manasseh. I noticed it because I wondered why you didn't put some of the wine on a piece of cloth at the end of a stick and hand it up to Caleb.'

'Well?' Manasseh asked. 'Isn't that just what I did?'

'But *you* had a drink *before* sunset,' Gomer said. 'And I remember it for a distinct reason. You see, I thought of asking you for some. You were drinking sure enough, Manasseh. But it wasn't from the wineskin. It was from a small stone jar with a stopper in it.'

For a moment there was silence. When he now spoke, Caleb's voice assumed its former tone of authority.

'So tell the truth, Manasseh,' he called out. 'I order you to do so before God. The wine was drugged, was it not?'

I decided I must intervene.

'Manasseh is my servant,' I said. And I was dismayed to find that my voice was shaking. 'I will not allow him to be questioned by anyone as if he were a criminal.'

But Caleb seemed unaware of my interruption. His eyes were gazing steadily at Manasseh.

'Before God, Manasseh,' Caleb cried out. 'Before God – was the wine drugged?'

Manasseh's worn face turned to me in defeat. I knew that it was no longer possible for him to lie.

'Yes,' Manasseh replied.

Caleb swung round to me.

'So there is your answer, Joseph,' he said bitterly.

At that instant my rage was so acute I could feel a fierce throbbing in my head. Suddenly the room became obscure and distorted. The lamp seemed to sway. I felt sick with giddiness. But passion swept my words forwards.

'Is it? Is that the answer you want? Because you cannot face responsibility any more?' I shouted out in fury to Caleb. 'Then listen to the truth. Listen to it. Yes, indeed, there were drugs in the wine. I studied medicine. I *knew* the drugs to ease your suffering and let you die in peace. I put those drugs in the wine. They had the effect I expected. An hour after you had drunk from the sponge you lost consciousness. One hour later – you were dead. You were dead when Manasseh and I took you down from the cross. The centurion was there to witness the fact. You were dead when we laid you in the tomb. It was when we unwound the sheet from your body that the miracle took place before our own eyes.'

'Then why did Manasseh try to lie?' Caleb asked.

'Because I ordered him to,' I replied.

'Why did *you* lie to me?' Caleb asked.

'As I said just now, truth sometimes runs along dark alleys,' I answered. 'I believed there was no need for any doubt. I am still sure of it.'

'You are the Messiah, dear Lord,' Leah stated. 'You are the Chosen One of Israel.'

Caleb took three steps towards Manasseh.

'Am I?' he demanded. 'Am I the Messiah?'

'How can Manasseh tell?' Leah exclaimed.

'Because he is a sincere man who fears God,' Caleb replied. And he turned back to Manasseh who was standing rigidly before him. 'Manasseh, am I standing here because of a miracle?' he asked. 'Or because of a mixture of drugs and a carefully made plot?'

Manasseh remained silent. His worn face was grim. Caleb looked towards Ben and Gomer.

'So there is the final answer,' Caleb said.

Manasseh turned to me. 'May I go, Master?' he asked.

'Yes, Manasseh,' I replied. And he went out.

Leah moved towards Caleb.

'You *are* the Messiah,' she insisted. 'You must be.'

'No, Leah,' Caleb answered.

'Then what are you?' Leah demanded.

Caleb was silent for a moment before he spoke.

'A man,' he answered, 'an ordinary man who once had prophetic gifts.'

'That is what he tells you for his own reasons,' I said.

'No, it's not possible,' Leah replied. Her face was puckered in consternation. Suddenly her expression changed, and I could see that some new thought had entered her mind. Staring at Caleb, Leah shook her head accusingly. 'Then you can't be Caleb,' Leah cried. Suddenly she swung round to Gomer and Ben. 'That's it, don't you see?' she demanded. 'He's not really Caleb. He's an impostor. Or some devil who has taken on his likeness.'

'He is Caleb,' Ben said quietly.

'Yes, Ben,' Caleb replied. 'I am Caleb – and no more than that.'

'And you are not the One foretold by the prophets?' Ben asked.

'No,' Caleb answered. 'I am now sure I am not.'

'But Master,' Gomer began tremulously, his plump face shining with sweat, 'if you are not the Chosen One, then are we no longer your disciples? Will nothing that you told us come to pass? Will we not be the first to enter the groves you spoke about – the fragrant groves of Paradise where the brooks run softly under palm trees all clustered with dates? Will we never see the fields where the wheat grows as high as the cedars of Lebanon? And the vineyards, shining with heavy bunches of grapes?'

'One day you will enter Paradise, Gomer,' Caleb said. 'I am sure of that. But it will not be yet.'

'But until then?' Gomer asked. 'What are we to do until then?'

'You must do what you think right in your heart,' Caleb replied.

'Then you are no longer our Master?' Gomer asked.

'No longer,' Caleb answered.

'Then are we not to spread your teaching?' Ben asked.

Caleb was silent. The corner of his mouth was twitching.

'No longer,' Caleb replied.

'The funds,' Gomer said. 'Remember I told you about the money.'

'I trust you, Gomer,' Caleb replied. 'I trust you to distribute the money among the disciples who are in need, for several of them have given up their work for my sake. Distribute it fairly.' Caleb tried to smile. 'But do not forget yourself,' he added.

'Thank you, Master,' Gomer mumbled.

Suddenly Leah gave a ghastly shriek of fear. Frantically, she stumbled towards Caleb. Her left hand was pointing, trembling, to her right arm which was now hanging down, rigid, at her side.

'Master, my arm,' she cried. 'My arm. I can't move it. I can't.'

Caleb looked down in dismay at the arm hanging stiffly by Leah's side. Then he took in a deep breath. He spoke firmly.

'Yes, Leah,' he said. 'You can indeed move it.'

'I can't, I tell you.'

'Try, Leah,' Caleb ordered.

I could see Leah's shoulders stretch in an effort to move her arm. But the arm remained rigid and motionless.

'It won't move,' she cried to him in a low moan. 'Please help me. Please.'

I longed to be able to help her, but there was nothing I could do. The force of her faith in Caleb had somehow removed the paralysis in her arm. Her faith had suddenly left her, and the arm was paralysed once more.

'Listen to me, Leah,' Caleb said. 'I will touch the skin of your arm, and then you will be able to move it. You will be cured as you were last time.'

'Yes,' Leah sighed. 'Like last time.'

Leah moved closer to him. Then, as Gomer and Ben watched in astonishment, Caleb stretched out his hand and grasped her wrist and held it firmly. He was breathing heavily. After a while, he withdrew his hand.

'Now move your arm, Leah,' he commanded. 'Move your arm.'

'Yes,' Leah whispered. 'I am trying.'

Leah was staring down at her arm. Her face was contorted by the effort she was making, but the arm remained motionless. Desperately she looked up at Caleb.

'Tell me that you're he,' she urged. 'Tell me that you're the Messiah. I know you are really. But just let me hear you say it. Then I'll be able to move my arm. I'm sure I will. Tell me that you're the Messiah. Tell me, Master.'

Caleb stared at her in silence. His blue eyes were again misted.

'I cannot,' he said.

'Why not?' Leah implored.

'Tell her the truth, Caleb,' I cried. 'You arose from the dead. You *are* the Messiah.'

In silence Caleb lowered his head.

'But why can't you?' Leah moaned. 'Why?'

'Because it would not be true,' Caleb answered.

'It would,' Leah wailed. 'It would.'

'No, Leah,' Caleb said in a whisper.

Once again Leah examined her arm. She gave a convulsive shudder. Suddenly Leah jerked up her head at Caleb.

'Caleb the prophet healed me,' she screamed at him. 'I was healed by Caleb, the Messiah, I tell you. I was healed, and I could move my arm like anyone else. My arm was made right again. I wasn't deformed any more. I was like any other woman. Better than many, in fact. And I'd got a chance. I could have found a good man to marry me. But now you have destroyed my arm, and it's deformed again. You've destroyed it – because you're not Caleb, I know it. Caleb was the Messiah. He told us so. He was the Anointed One. Caleb was the Son of the Living God. He was fine and beautiful, brave and strong. But you're not Caleb. You're a devil, a devil, an evil, grey-haired devil. And I hate you. I revile you. I spit on you. I spit on you.'

I moved across to Leah and put my arm on her shoulder.

'Leah,' I murmured softly. 'Leah.'

She turned and peered up at me through her tears. All the love I had felt for her when I had been a child now came back to me.

'He's a devil, I tell you,' she wailed. 'Send him away. Please, Master. Please find Caleb. I need Caleb. Oh God, I need Caleb. Send me Caleb.'

Then Leah fell down at my feet, sobbing violently.

'Please, Master,' she entreated.

I tried to comfort her, but her cries had become hysterical. At that moment I could not leave the room. However, I knew that Leah was fond of Ben, and I turned to him.

'Ben, please look after her,' I said.

Gently, Ben helped Leah to her feet.

'Ben will take you downstairs,' I told Leah. 'I will be down presently. I shall soon be with you.'

Ben helped Leah to the door. Caleb sat down at the table, his head in his hands. I did not see his face. I turned to Gomer.

'You and Ben should go back to Galilee separately,' I told him.

Gomer nodded. He was too distressed to speak.

'I will travel to Galilee after the meeting of the Sanhedrin tomorrow,' I continued. 'So I will be there if you need me.'

I went to the window and drew aside the curtains and looked out. The alley seemed deserted.

'I think you should leave now, Gomer,' I announced.

'Yes, Excellency,' Gomer replied.

Slowly he approached the table at which Caleb was sitting. I could see that Gomer was close to despair.

'Master,' he began nervously. And Caleb looked up at him. 'When will I see you again?' Gomer asked.

'Soon, I hope, Gomer,' Caleb said.

'Perhaps you will decide to come in secret to Galilee, when you're strong?' Gomer enquired with a last flicker of hopefulness.

'It will not be for a while,' Caleb answered.

'You're not angry with me?' Gomer asked. It was a plea more than a question.

'No, Gomer,' Caleb replied.

'I mean, am I completely forgiven?' Gomer's flabby face was now shivering with intensity.

'Yes,' Caleb said. 'You are completely forgiven.'

'I will collect the funds from Manny, of course,' Gomer said in a tremulous voice. 'I'll use the money as you said. But it would help – I mean, if I knew you'd be back on some definite date, that would help me. Temptation's always there in this life, if you see what I mean.'

'You will find strength to resist it,' Caleb told him.

'I hope so, I do hope so. But it's going to be hard now.' Gomer broke off in confusion. 'But I'll do my best, I promise,' he continued. 'Yes, I can safely say so.'

Gomer glanced anxiously around the room as if he had forgotten something.

'Well, I'll be off,' he said in his shaky voice. 'So there it is . . . We can only try our best. We can't do any more.'

Gomer joined his hands together in salutation.

'Goodbye, Excellency,' he said to me quaveringly. 'Goodbye, Master. I will see you one of these days. I mean, that's what I hope.'

'Goodbye, Gomer,' Caleb said. 'Go in peace.'

With his head bent as if he were carrying a heavy load on his shoulder, and with his greasy face now set stolidly in resignation as if he were convinced that he must carry that load for all eternity, Gomer dragged his gross body from the room.

I was left alone with Caleb.

I went to the table and poured myself some wine, and drank it in a gulp.

'Poor Caleb,' I said to him.

Caleb stared at me with his misted eyes.

'There was a time when I would have been too proud to accept your pity,' Caleb said after a pause. 'But now I am grateful for it, because I need your help. I must leave Jerusalem. I must leave very soon. As I told you, I am sick in my mind. I can abide these walls no longer. Please help me to go – for good and for ever.'

'I say "poor Caleb" because I am enraged with you,' I told him. 'I am angered because you have wrecked part of my design. But I cannot hate you, for the truth is I took to you from the moment we first met. I am still devoted to you, Caleb. So, of course I will help you. As we both know, I have made plans for you to leave for Egypt tonight when the convoy returns to Alexandria. They are all Egyptians, so there is no danger you will be recognized. I will come down and visit you as soon as I can leave Jerusalem. It is a small house by the harbour. You will find peace there – and strength.'

'No,' Caleb said.

'I was trained as a doctor, Caleb,' I told him. 'You are young. I am sure you will soon be well again.'

'I am not going to Alexandria,' Caleb said.

'Why not?' I demanded. 'Certainly you cannot return to Galilee'.

'Do not worry. I will not cause you trouble,' Caleb replied. 'I will take your convoy south until I reach the desert. Then I will leave it.'

'But why?' I asked. 'Do you not wish to go to Alexandria?'

'I am not certain what I want to do,' Caleb answered. 'But one thing I do know. I need to be in the wilderness for a while.'

'Would it not be wiser to recover your strength in the seclusion of my house in Alexandria – and then perhaps travel in the desert or visit the Essenes?'

'I must go to the wilderness,' Caleb replied.

'But when shall I see you again?' I asked.

'Are you sure you want to see me, Joseph?' Caleb enquired.

'Very sure.'

Caleb contemplated me with a strange look – as if he was in possession of some knowledge that was denied to me.

'Why do you want to see me again?' Caleb asked.

I spoke hurriedly to conceal the desperate urgency behind my words.

'For many reasons,' I told him. 'Let me be honest. I am indeed very fond of you, so listen to me, Caleb. Do not make any decision as yet. Wander in the wilderness for a while. You have done so before. You know how to live there. But while you are wandering, remember there is a house in Alexandria waiting for you, with servants to look after you. I will send word to them to expect the arrival of a friend of mine at any time in the next few weeks or so. You can easily find the house. The harbour master will tell you where it is. So I hope I will see you there.'

There was a silence. As Caleb looked at me, it suddenly seemed to me that I could detect a part of his nature, perhaps an instinct, which was almost certainly unknown to him. This deep-buried instinct was now urging him to abandon all effort in his life to struggle against the waves that still dashed over him. This instinct had produced a profound wish to submit once and for all, and to deliver himself to the warm waters of peace and security. I could sense his longing for complete passivity; I was very much aware of his desire to be at last set free from his conscience and to be entirely dominated. I could imagine the moment when I could finally achieve this freedom for him. But as Caleb watched me, his eyes suddenly widened in distrust as if I had menaced him.

'What about Raguel?' Caleb asked.

'Why should you care about Raguel?' I enquired in surprise.

'Raguel has very little remaining to him,' Caleb said after a pause. 'But he still has one thing left.'

'His self-pity?' I suggested. And immediately I felt ashamed for my disloyalty.

'No, Joseph,' Caleb answered, his eyes now gazing at me calmly in the sureness of his conviction. 'His love for you.'

I gaped at Caleb in amazement.

'For that reason alone we should not meet in Egypt,' Caleb continued gently. 'But if you want to help me, Joseph, let me go with your caravan as far as the desert. And if you want to be very kind to me, please could you give me a coat – because it gets very cold in the desert at nights.'

For a moment I still remained staring at Caleb in bewilderment while the words he had spoken hammered in my brain. I could not wholly comprehend the meaning of what he had said. It was as if I myself had not been present in the room, and the words had been spoken to some stranger. I could not bring my disordered mind to understand what had occurred.

'Do not worry, Caleb,' I heard myself saying. 'I have got everything prepared for your journey.'

But I knew that I was only speaking to comfort myself. I felt a heavy throbbing in my head.

'I shall go with them as far as the desert,' Caleb repeated quietly.

Then, at last, with a lurch of misery, I knew I was utterly defeated. My plan had failed, and I had lost Caleb. I had lost the only person whom I could have loved both with respect and passion. He had eluded me. Caleb was leaving. And I had a definite presentiment I would never see him again. This was the last time we would ever be together. If that were so, I told myself, I did not wish to remember the sorrowful face of the person who now watched me in distress, with dull blue eyes from across the room. I wanted to be able to recollect the young man, cheerful, virile, and beautiful, who had entered my house that morning in Galilee – long ago, many ages ago, it seemed. I wanted to recall the smooth and lovely youth, poised and graceful and dazzling. Accordingly, I moved towards him, and, as a blind man might, I raised my hand and put my palm against his cheek, so that I could feel the warmth of him and his wonderful softness for the last time.

But my eyes were open, and in horror I beheld the scared look of complete revulsion on his face – and then the sudden change of expression. With a violent wrench of my head, I turned away from Caleb's gaze of tender compassion.

CHAPTER SEVEN

I must think of all that Caleb said to me. I am tired. But I must repeat his words. I must repeat to myself the words he spoke to me – before I forget them.

I had tended to Leah as best I could.

'Ben,' she kept muttering to me, 'please, Ben, find me the *real* Caleb.'

But gradually her fit subsided and she grew calmer.

I was in the hall when Master Joseph hurried down the stairs. He was panting, and his hands were trembling. I had never seen him so agitated. But what worried me most of all was the look in his eyes. It was a look of hatred mixed with terror. I knew that Master Joseph sometimes had fits of anger, but this was more serious. He seemed almost mad. When he saw me he stopped and glared at me.

'What is it, Ben?' he asked.

'Leah is quieter now,' I told him. 'I think she will sleep very soon.'

'Good,' Master Joseph muttered. 'I will go to see her presently. But first I must find the things Caleb will need for his journey. The caravan should nearly be ready. You had better go upstairs and say goodbye to him.'

I climbed the stairs to the living-room, moving slowly because I wanted time to think. The Master was standing by the table at the window. The curtains were still partly drawn back, and he was staring out at the night. As I came into the room he turned round. He tried to give me a smile.

'Where are you going, Master?' I asked.

'For what seems a long time, I have been shut in the four walls of my room,' Caleb answered me. 'I want to be in an open space. I want to feel the wind against my forehead, and see the stars above my head. So I will wander.'

'But you need someone to look after you,' I said quietly. 'Please, Master, let me go with you.'

'You do not understand, Ben,' Caleb replied. 'I am not worth it. I am just the son of a man with a vineyard in Cana and of his wife from the same village. You must no longer call me "Master".'

'You will always be my Master,' I answered. 'And also my guide.'

'I have nowhere to guide you,' he replied.

'God will come back to you,' I said. 'So will your strength. Your teaching will yet succeed.'

'No, Ben,' he replied. 'My teaching will never succeed. And I can tell you why. Because my message appealed only to the poor and the outcasts. I never appealed to the rich and powerful. On the contrary, my teaching menaced their position. So I was condemned and crucified. I was not condemned because I was wrong but because my preaching was not successful enough. If I had been a success my message would have been thought correct. But the man who fails is considered to have done something wrong. The man who is poor is suspected of being a criminal. The man who is sick is believed to have committed a sin.'

I was shocked to hear the bitterness in Caleb's voice. He turned away from the window and stood by one of the lamps, looking at it as if he could read some other message from its flame.

'No religion can succeed unless it appeals to those in power, unless it is attractive to authority,' he continued. 'So no religion will prevail unless it persuades men that the God they must worship has blessed those in authority over them. God, they must be told, is on the side of Valerius Gratus, our Governor. He is on the side of Caiaphas, the High Priest. God supports each member of the Sanhedrin. He helps every rich Pharisee, Sadducee, and Scribe. God, they must be told, loves rich, powerful men. He cares nothing for the poor and weak.'

'But Master,' I said, 'you could never believe in such a God.'

'God has left me,' he answered. 'I do not know God any longer. If God exists, I can only surmise about him. Perhaps there was a God who created the world. Perhaps there was a God who created the sun and the moon and the earth we live on. Perhaps this God did create mountains and lakes, hills, plains and seas. Perhaps it was he who created Man. But soon after that time, I believe, God began to lose his power. And by now he has lost all control over the world he created.'

'But God who made all the earth cannot be weak,' I said.

'If he is not weak, *then* what kind of God is he? I will tell you, Ben,' he cried. 'A God who is concerned only to perpetuate his glory, to maintain his control, to keep in power, to sit firmly on the throne at any price. He does not care much about the shape of the world. Let stars fall. Let mountains slide down into the sea. Stars and mountains are of no account. Forests and deserts do not matter. Nor birds, nor beasts – for *they* cannot glorify him. Only Man can do that. Only Man can sing his praises at morning and noon and night. So Man must be preserved by any means. The race of mankind must not die out. So God has implanted a grain of lust in each one of us. Each one of us has the grain implanted so that, inexorably, more children are born, and one generation succeeds another. And if people grow too numerous to feed, they can be destroyed by war or pestilence. For God is without mercy. God is ruthless. God is cruel.'

Then he turned away from the lamp, and I suppose he must have seen from my face how upset and disturbed his words had made me.

'But I no longer know,' he said. 'I am not sure any longer. I have no authority. So do not look sad, Ben, for all I say may be wrong.'

'I am sad because you grieve,' I replied. 'God may have left you for a time. But you have friends. All the same, you are still not strong. You mustn't be alone. Not for some while at least, so let me come with you on your journey. I can do so with a good conscience. I haven't told you, Master, but my wife Rachel has gone back to her parents. In fact, she wants to be rid of me. So I can go with you, Master. I'm also alone, and I need you.'

He stretched out his arms towards me, and then let them fall to his side.

'Look at me as I am now,' he cried. 'How can you need me?'

'I don't understand,' I replied.

Suddenly the corner of Caleb's mouth began to quiver, and he put up his hand to conceal it.

'I would like you to come with me,' he said. 'Whatever kind of life it was, I would be happy with you as a companion on the way. But I can't – I can't help you any more . . . I cannot help anyone, Ben.'

'Let me come with you,' I entreated. 'Let *me* try to help *you* for once. Please let me.'

'No, Ben,' he said. 'You must go back to Galilee. Go and visit your wife at her parents' house. You will find she will welcome you – for I am certain she loves you.'

As he stood watching me he tried to smile.

'She *must* love you,' he added. 'So ask her to return to your house.'

Suddenly I realized that he might be going away from me for good. I moved towards him desperately. The words came tumbling out of my mouth.

'I can't leave you,' I told him. 'You are all my life to me. How can I live without you?'

'You will live,' he said quietly. 'You will have children. And when you watch them playing in the sunshine you will rejoice. And I will visit you – and then I too will rejoice.'

'Let me go with you,' I pleaded. 'Just for a little while?'

'No, Ben,' he answered. 'This journey I must make alone.'

'Then promise you will visit me soon.'

'As soon as I can.'

'Each evening when I'm out with the boat,' I said, 'each evening I will pray to God to bring you back to me.'

'Oh, Ben,' he said in a hoarse whisper.

Suddenly he turned away from me. He walked over to the window and looked out again. When he next spoke, his voice was once more calm.

'Come and watch,' he said. 'We may not see the peace of the night together for some time.'

I went and stood beside him at the window. He was silent, and I felt he was recalling the weeks when his lack of strength had forced him to confine himself to the room upstairs. During those days he must have had time to think about his teaching and to consider his failure. However, he was still a wonderful person – even though, for a while, God might have abandoned him. I certainly believed that he was inspired. As if he had understood my thoughts, he spoke.

'Sometimes I can still feel the throb of the world,' he said. 'Moreover, although I have lost the spirit that guided my life, I can still use my mind, I can still contemplate the infinite loveliness of some of the things that are around us.'

Once again he was silent, and I knew that his mind was far away.

'Now I come to look back,' he continued, 'I realize that we own nothing in life. Each day we live is lent to us from the moment we are born. So let us accept what has been lent to us. Let us think, while we still have minds. Let us love, while we still have hearts. Let us admire beauty, while we can see, and music, while we can still hear. Let us enjoy all the blessings life can lend us. And when we die, let us pray that we will not be blamed for our enjoyment of the good things we have found on earth – among so many sad ones.'

'Where will you go?' I asked again.

'When I was young, I could always find peace in wandering,' he told me. 'I will wander again. There are villages in the country where I can find shelter . . . And tents in the desert.'

He glanced at me with a slight smile.

'You stare at me, Ben. Have I changed so very much?' he asked.

'No,' I answered. And it was true. Now that I was alone with him, I felt he was the same person I had met by the lake and loved so dearly.

'But my words have changed?' he demanded. 'Yes, I suppose they have. But I am lost. I turn on to various paths which I hope will lead me to the truth. In addition, I sometimes contradict myself. It is the way of my mind. But, in essence, I still pray for the same things. If there is a God, I can only pray he will reward the poor and the sick, the gentle and the humble. Above all, I pray he will bless those who, because of their limitations, are unable to share in the feast of life and who can only watch – as the plates in the brightly-lit room are taken away, one by one.'

He turned away from the window and gazed at me. I knew that he was examining me so intently because he wanted to remember me until the day we met again. From below I heard the sound of footsteps in the courtyard.

'I ought to go,' I said.

He nodded. When he spoke, his voice was so quiet I could hardly hear him.

'In my spirit I shall carry you with me,' he told me. 'I shall for ever.'

The door opened, and Master Joseph came in. Immediately he appeared I saw that he had regained his air of authority. The almost insane expression had left his face. He was once again the man I had known and admired in Galilee.

'All is ready for the journey,' he announced.

I moved towards the door, then stopped.

'Goodbye, Master Joseph,' I mumbled.

Joseph nodded to me, and I turned to Caleb.

'Goodbye, Master,' I managed to blurt out.

Caleb looked at me in silence. Then raised his right hand into the air.

'Peace be with you, Ben,' he said.

And I walked out of the room.

All the way back from Jerusalem to Galilee I thought about it. I thought about what he had said and about what he had told me to do. But I had a worry all of my own. I knew that if – as Caleb had told me I should – I persuaded Rachel to come back to live with me in the house I still shared with my father, her presence, in time, would probably comfort me. But Rachel was my wife. And accordingly – and quite naturally – she would expect me to make love to her. And, knowing Rachel as I did, I was sure that she would expect it to be the very night of her return to the house. And I was worried, because I was afraid the sadness I felt might destroy my vigour.

However, the truth is that when it comes to making love, the mind is one thing, and the body is another. My mind, when we went to our room earlier this evening, was filled with sad thoughts and terrible visions. But later, as I held Rachel in my arms and felt her pressing against me, my body began to stir all of its own – as if I had nothing to do with it, and it was no part of me.

Rachel is now happy and asleep. She is my wife, and I can still love her. But before I sleep I must think of everything he said to me – six evenings ago – I must repeat it all to myself again before I forget it.

Each night that I am out fishing I will pray to God. And surely God must bring him back to me.

CHAPTER EIGHT

My feelings towards Caleb had diminished my self-respect both as a person and as a senator; I must now recover my zest for living and my dignity.

My fit of rage – certainly it was no more serious than an outburst of anger – was finished. I was now resigned to the fact that Caleb was leaving me for good. My passion for him, I could now realize, had been inflamed only because my attraction to him coincided with my political ambition. Fortunately my central plan had in no way been compromised. My immediate concern was for Caleb to leave Jerusalem. Then I could devote myself to the problem of Raguel.

'The convoy leader will soon be ready,' I told Caleb. 'He has got all you will require.'

'Thank you, Joseph,' Caleb replied.

'I do not need to ask you to keep secret all that has recently happened – for your sake and mine,' I said. 'And from your words a while ago, I presume I am correct in assuming we will not meet again?'

Caleb looked at me with the deep blue eyes I had once admired, but which were now haunted and dim.

'Yes,' he replied. 'Though I believe in a way it has been your decision.'

I could not understand the purpose of his remark. But it no longer mattered. I had only one last thing to say to him.

'On your wanderings, Caleb, commune with your soul and work with your mind,' I told him. 'But remember that the letter of your life which you write each day is enclosed by a scroll of flesh. And the seal has now been broken.'

When I saw Caleb flinch I knew my words had struck their mark.

'I will not forget,' Caleb answered. 'Memory I still have – even if I can seldom find courage to use it.'

Raguel entered the room as Caleb spoke. I had been expecting him for some time.

'I came here with the Egyptian officer,' Raguel explained to Caleb, evidently feeling he must apologize for his arrival. 'The convoy is ready.'

Caleb stood in silence, watching Raguel most attentively, as if his presence could somehow instruct him in an important lesson.

'I am leaving with the convoy,' Caleb told Raguel after a pause. 'But not for Egypt. Only as far as the desert.'

Raguel glanced at me in surprise. 'I thought you were travelling to Alexandria,' he said.

'No,' Caleb replied.

Raguel now looked at once suspicious and puzzled.

'Why not?' he asked. 'I thought it had all been planned.'

'Joseph made the decision,' Caleb answered before I could speak.

Raguel stared at me. 'Why the sudden change?' he enquired.

'You know why, Raguel,' Caleb told him.

'Do I?' Raguel demanded.

'Surely,' Caleb replied.

Raguel was looking at Caleb in bewilderment.

'You have no hatred for me, have you?' he asked. But his tone of voice made it sound more like a statement than a question.

'No,' Caleb answered quietly. Then he moved towards me.

'Goodbye, Joseph,' Caleb said. 'I am grateful to you for your help.'

Raguel was still staring at him.

'Have you no hatred in you?' Raguel asked.

'None for anything I can understand,' Caleb replied.

There was a knock at the door, and Manasseh came in. Ordinarily he would not have knocked before entering, but since the night we had brought Caleb to the house his habit had changed. Manasseh would be thankful when Caleb had finally left and we could resume our usual way of life once again.

'The officer is waiting for you,' he said to Caleb.

'Thank you, Manasseh,' Caleb replied. And I could see that he was about to say more, so I interrupted.

'You need not take farewell of Manasseh now,' I told Caleb. 'He will go with you to the Valley Gate.'

Manasseh nodded to me and left the room, leaving the door open.

Caleb joined his hands and raised them in salutation, first to Raguel, and then to me.

'Peace be with you both,' he said.

His voice was calm, and held not a tinge of regret that he was leaving behind him part of his life and his whole mission. But in the tone of his voice there was implicit a complete and utter resignation of all that had once been of such intense importance to him.

'Peace be with you,' Caleb repeated.

Then he turned away from us and walked out of the room.

I was left alone with Raguel.

There was silence. Slowly Raguel crossed the room and sat down in a chair next to the table. I was about to say something to break the strain of our silence – when Raguel began talking in the light, almost flippant, tone of voice he sometimes uses to discuss serious matters. Immediately I realized he was speaking only in order to conceal his embarrassment.

'I suppose a religion must *one day* come which will capture all mankind,' Raguel began. 'After all, until now, religions have appealed only to the good men of the world – or to wicked men if they will consent to be converted from their evil ways. But the masses of people are both good and evil. So I would say that the only religion that has any hope of sweeping across the world would be a religion which recognizes that mankind is both sensual and idealistic, trivial and serious, cruel and kind, selfish and full of altruism. Above all it must accept the fact that mankind is mainly swayed by self-interest.'

I had listened to Raguel attentively. I now nodded my head although I did not agree with him. Again there was silence. Suddenly Raguel leaned forward.

'Was it true what Caleb said?' he asked. 'Did you really change your mind?'

At that stage I did not wish the conversation to become awkwardly earnest. I smiled gently at Raguel.

'As I keep telling you, my dear Raguel, truth runs along dark alleys,' I replied. 'So please may I ask you to put your question differently?'

Raguel smiled back at me. I could see that he, too, was glad that we need not be over-serious.

'How should I phrase it then?' he asked. And for the first time there was a hint of amusement in his eyes.

'You could ask if I am glad that Caleb has left for good,' I suggested.

'Are you glad he has gone, Joseph?' Raguel asked.

'Yes,' I answered.

Raguel rose from his chair and wandered across to the table. Idly he picked up the little wooden cross that Manasseh had brought me.

'May I ask why you are glad?' he enquired.

'Because I do not want to lose you,' I told him.

'Are you certain, Joseph?' he asked.

'Yes, I am certain,' I answered. 'Will you stay with me, Raguel?'

'I suppose so,' he replied.

Suddenly, the oppression that had weighed down my spirit vanished, and I felt almost light-hearted.

'I think we should leave Jerusalem as soon as we can,' I said to Raguel. 'It holds bad memories for us both. Where would you like us to go?'

'Well,' Raguel began slowly, thinking aloud. 'Should we go back to Galilee? No – that could still be dangerous . . . Jericho? No – we would have to face all the problems of your estate there, and we would never be alone together . . . What about that crumbling old house which belonged to your father? You never seem to go there.'

As Raguel spoke I could see the old house. First, there was the large outer courtyard of grey stone with an elaborate fountain and rooms surrounding it. An archway led to a second courtyard with rooms where there was complete privacy. I could see the fine wood of the furniture with its beautiful ivory inlays. I could see the high beds and tall chests, the gold and silver ornaments, and the long wooden tables. And outside I could see the willows drooping over the stream that ran through the end of the garden, and beyond, the orange groves. And below the tranquil mansion, far below, was the village, with flat-roofed stone houses tumbling down the hillside, each with its little garden, fresh and green. I could see the narrow, cobbled streets winding down into the valley, and the wide plains in the distance.

'But the place is very quiet,' I told Raguel. 'I am afraid you might find it dull.'

'I want us to settle down alone together once again,' Raguel said. Though his voice was serious, I could not help being afraid that this sudden desire for solitude might perhaps be one of Raguel's whims.

'If we went to Arimathaea, and I opened up the old house there,' I said, 'would you really stay with me, Raguel? Would you make an effort, as I would, to try to establish a completely new life together?'

'Yes, Joseph, I promise you,' Raguel answered. And I knew that his reply was sincere. He seemed happy, and I was pleased.

'And would you stay with me for good in Arimathaea?' I asked.

Raguel was gazing down at the wooden cross which he was twisting round in the fingers of his right hand. I wondered if he had heard my last question, for he appeared to be absorbed in some thought which seemed to have occurred to him as I had spoken. To judge from the distant yet quite hopeful expression in his eyes, his thought lay in the future.

'For good, Raguel?' I repeated.

Raguel put down the cross on to the table.

'Yes,' he replied.

Then Raguel glanced up at me with a sad smile.

'Or until yet another young preacher comes along,' he added.